A TOUCH OF MAGIC

Two Nocturne Falls Universe Stories

SELA CARSEN

*Katherine,
Love the magic
of Nocturne Falls!
Sela Carsen
Silke Campor*

Dear Reader,

Nocturne Falls has become a magical place for so many people, myself included. Over and over I've heard from you that it's a town you'd love to visit and even live in! I can tell you that writing the books is just as much fun for me.

With your enthusiasm for the series in mind – and your many requests for more books – the Nocturne Falls Universe was born. It's a project near and dear to my heart, and one I am very excited about.

I hope these new, guest-authored books will entertain and delight you. And best of all, I hope they allow you to discover some great new authors! (And if you like this book, be sure to check out the rest of the Nocturne Falls Universe offerings.)

For more information about the Nocturne Falls Universe, visit http://kristenpainter.com/sugar-skull-books/

In the meantime, happy reading!

Kristen Painter

MAGIC'S SONG:

A Nocturne Falls Universe Story
MAGIC'S FATE:
A Nocturne Falls Universe Story
Copyright © 2017 by Sela Carsen

All rights reserved. No part of this book may be reproduced in any form or by any electronic or mechanical means, including information storage and retrieval systems—except in the case of brief quotations embodied in critical articles or reviews—without permission in writing from the author.

This book is a work of fiction and was made possible by a special agreement with Sugar Skull Books, but hasn't been reviewed or edited by Kristen Painter. All characters, events, scenes, plots and associated elements appearing in the original Nocturne Falls series remain the exclusive copyrighted and/or trademarked property of Kristen Painter, Sugar Skull Books and their affiliates or licensors.

Any similarity to real person, living or dead, is purely coincidental and not intended by the author or Sugar Skull Books.

Published in the United States of America.

Magic's Song

Prologue

THE KELPIE

The kelpie raised his head and sent out a mournful whinny.

These weren't his native shores and he was lonely. No nixies, no selkies, not a bean nighe in sight. No blue men from the Minch, or boobries from the lochs of Argyllshire, not even one of his Shetland cousins, a Tangie. He scraped his hooves against the frost-killed grass and nibbled at it forlornly.

Looking for something more than drowning unsuspecting travelers, he'd fled the Unseelie Court of Scotland and ended up in this land far across the seas. But he was alone here.

Until he found a herd of his own, whether it was fae, animal, or even human, he roamed this creek filled with magic, and waited for a friend.

Chapter One

*T*rick Scanlon parked his motorcycle at the edge of the wide creek after passing a sign that read "Welcome to Nocturne Falls – Where Every Day is Halloween!" He looked around to see if anyone else was there. No one. Blessed peace, and plenty of quiet now that he'd killed the heavy bike's engine. He pulled off his helmet and walked over to the water's edge, then closed his eyes.

In the dimming winter afternoon, he breathed in the clean, fresh flowing stream, the crisp scent of the cold in the air, the damp earth giving beneath his boots. A far cry from the long roads and endless touring he did now. Singing to sold out crowds of country music fans, grateful as he was, hadn't left him space to just be and breathe in far too long.

He stood for a few minutes, letting the winter breeze blow away a little more of the pressure that rode him like he rode his old Triumph.

In the stillness, a lonesome whinny drew him further into the thicket surrounding the creek until he spotted the horse. Black as sin, its coat glistened and shone, even on such a cloudy day. It nickered again, shaking its head at him, and Trick moved closer.

He wasn't really familiar with horses unless they were in a motor, but if the animal was lost or hurt, then he'd try to help.

He crept closer until he was near enough to touch. Heat billowed off the animal and its coat was wet, as if it had been in the water. It didn't have any kind of bridle or halter, so he had no idea how to lead it.

"I'm sorry I don't have an apple or anything for you."

The horse rubbed its face along his shoulder, knocking him back a half step.

"All right, all right. Let's see if we can't get you back to the road and into town. Maybe I can find out who you belong to." He didn't recall seeing any ranches or horse farms along the way, but surely someone would know where this magnificent animal came from.

Trick traced a hand down its warm, damp neck for a quick pat, then tried to turn to find the best path leading back to the road. Tried to, because his hand was stuck.

"What the...?" He pulled harder, and though his hand slid across the horse's neck, his fingers refused to rise from its coat.

Trick stared, startled, into the horse's dark eye and he swore the thing winked. Like it was going to have a really good time dragging him to hell.

The large animal bumped into his side, knocking him off balance again, so he was forced to put his other hand higher on its back. He was completely screwed now. Both hands were stuck to the horse, and there was no way to keep up as it began to dance, high stepping back and forth like it was in some kind of show event.

With no real choice left, Trick hauled himself up on the horse's back and tucked his knees up to keep his tender parts

Magic's Song

from hammering against its spine. He'd seen plenty of trouble in his life, but this was a whole new level of messed up.

"You want to tell me where we're going?" he yelled.

The horse reared up, neighing wildly, but Trick wasn't going anywhere. He was somehow glued to the horse's back as it galloped, not up to the road, but toward the water where it splashed and raced down the shallow creek bed.

The moon rose, bright and clear, showing Trick where they were headed. The creek widened into the large, dark circle of a pond a hundred yards across, but there was no telling how deep it ran. A litany of every foul word he'd ever learned in his time as an Army Ranger ran through his mind as he sucked in his breath.

"No! Nonononono!" The horse jumped, and Trick wished he'd had better final words as the water closed over his head. Of course, of all the ways he'd ever thought he'd die, magically glued to the back of a swimming devil horse was not on the list.

Under the surface, he struggled to break free. The horse touched bottom – deeper than he'd imagined a pond in a little creek could be – and pushed back up to the air. Trick gasped in a precious breath before they went down again.

It wasn't enough. His lungs were burning, and he realized he wasn't going to make it to his next concert in Atlanta. This was it. His muscles went slack, and he opened his eyes to take his last look around. As calm descended, he heard music, as if from heaven. In the dark water, he saw the figure of a woman swimming toward him.

Her mouth was open, and her clear, pure song enveloped him.

It was a gift, this song, and one he shared. It was a song he gave to others when he knew they needed it, something to cling to as they breathed their last. He'd sung this to his brothers in the desert so far from home. He'd given them this song as he held them while they died, and he'd given it to the ones who lived, too, to help them remember the ones they'd left behind who still loved them.

It was a song he'd heard his whole life. He'd learned it in his mother's womb, it had comforted him when he was sad, given him courage in the face of fear, and now it welcomed him as death stretched out its embrace.

Except he didn't die.

The horse surfaced, and Trick sucked air for dear life. As the animal made for shore at an unnatural speed, Trick coughed. Water burned like acid as it came flooding out of his mouth and nose.

The moment the horse leapt up onto the rocky bank, Trick came unstuck.

The horse stopped.

Trick didn't.

Slick, wet mane slid through his fingers and he had a brief, upside-down view of the horse's long, snickering face as he went flying over it.

He landed with a thud, and a thousand tiny, sharp rocks dug into his back. But he was pretty sure nothing was broken, and bruises were better than drowning.

He lay there, trying to remember how his lungs worked, and the horse leaned down to nose him, dripping cold water and blowing slime all over him.

He wiped a hand down his face, too shocked and out of breath to move away. "Demon pony. I hate you."

The horse lipped his collar.

"I don't care. I still don't like you."

"Oh, don't be that way. He was only playing with you."

Trick rolled to his side with painful effort, and blinked, hearing his angel's voice. She was in the water, hanging onto the rock overhang on the edge of the pond, her head resting on her crossed arms as she scolded the horse. "But you should know better. You can't play with people like that. You'll break one of them one of these days."

The horse whickered at her and shook his head.

"Less playing," Trick croaked, coughing up more creek. "More breathing." He pulled his exhausted, battered body closer to her.

In the gray light, her hair was a dark red cloud in the water, pouring over her shoulders and floating on tiny waves. Large, dark green eyes dominated her delicately sculpted face, and she hovered in the freezing water wearing a pretty bikini top without a care or even a shiver.

"Come out. You must be freezing." He opened his arms, but she shook her head.

"No, thank you." His angel was extremely polite, even as she retreated slightly. "I'm never cold in the water. Why were you playing with the kelpie?"

"The what?"

"The water horse. They're dangerous, you know."

"I do now. Was that you singing? I thought it was my 'have a good afterlife' music." Trick sat up fully, expecting to ache all over, but feeling better.

Miraculously better, in fact. He hurt a little, but nothing like what he should have after the ride from hell. In fact, little fizzes of something like music were only now fading in his body. Something very like what he sometimes felt when he sang. It popped and bubbled, taking away all his aches and pains, and he wanted to ask her to sing for him again.

She was smiling at him, sort of treading water in the middle of the pond, swimming back and forth a little. But when she leaned back and did a full roll, he saw it.

A mermaid's tail, glistening as she twisted it in the water. Her slender body subtly shifted to smooth wet scales, bright red with glimmers of gold. And at the end of her tail, a delicate, translucent fan of fins trailed in the water.

"Is that a costume? That looks so real. It's amazing."

That made her frown. She looked down at herself and her beautiful mermaid's tail. "Did you drink any of the water?"

"Lady, I drank half the pond. Why?" The horse stamped and snuffled behind him, and Trick glanced back. "Do you see this?" He must have hit his head. He was talking to a horse. Maybe hypothermia was setting in. Now that the shock had worn off, he was starting to shake. He wrapped his arms around his body and tried to contain the shudders.

A horse had tried to drown him. The woman in the pond was a mermaid.

If he hadn't already been sitting down, he'd have said he needed to sit down.

"You're human, aren't you?" she asked. "A tourist? Just passing through?"

He nodded, dumbly. How was he supposed to answer that? Of course he was human.

Suddenly, she covered herself, sinking down into the water until it came up to her chin. Too late. He'd already seen her.

"You need to leave," she said, a complete turnaround from her earlier, welcoming banter. "Don't come down to the water again. Not everything here is friendly."

"You can't be real."

Her shoulders slumped and he didn't think a mermaid should look so sad. "I'm glad you're alive. Go get dry and warm. And stay out of the water."

With a final wave, she turned away and dove deep, flipping her tail at him as she swam away.

DARIA FELT BAD, leaving that poor man all wet beside Nix's Pond, but what else could she do? She'd never met a human who didn't respond to the bespelled waters of Nocturne Falls before.

She was a *rusalka*, a Russian water fae, and her tail had never once been seen by a human. She nearly groaned.

This meant a meeting with Alice Bishop, the very powerful witch who'd laid the spell on Nocturne Falls, to tell her that she'd encountered someone who didn't respond to the enchantment. The water that ran from Wolf Creek, through Nix's Pond and down through the woods to the small, rocky falls was supposed to blur the edges of reality for human tourists who came to the town to enjoy its year-round kooky Halloween ambiance. Bottles of the bespelled water were sold in every shop to make sure strangers didn't accidentally see something they shouldn't – a fairy's wings, a werewolf's shift, or a gargoyle coming to life in the town square. Anything they happened to witness would either not register, or, given the kitschy tourist draw of the town, was explained away as a costume or a trick.

But he had ridden a kelpie and survived. And he definitely knew what she was. She'd seen the moment he realized her tail was not part of an elaborate costume.

She only knew that he was compelling in a way she hadn't encountered in far too long. He'd been long and lanky, but his wet T-shirt had displayed a nicely muscled chest and shoulders. His short dark hair was just long enough to have a little curl on the end where the water had dripped off. And the way those brown eyes had looked back at her made her crave dark chocolate. It didn't hurt that the man had cheekbones like a British movie star. She sighed a little. Yeah, he'd hit her happy buttons.

But reality intruded. The kelpie could be good news or bad. She hadn't seen him in her waters before, so she didn't know if he was traveling with the human, or if it had just been the man's bad luck to encounter the Unseelie beast.

Daria had learned about other worlds at her mother's knee. Other fae wouldn't care if she was ignorant of their ways, and even she knew the last thing anyone wanted to do was cross a member of the Scottish dark fae court. Caution would be her watchword around the kelpie, which brought to mind her other problem.

She was not looking forward to telling Alice her magic was wonky. The stern witch wasn't exactly the most welcoming person in town, probably a result of having nearly been burned at the stake during the Salem witch trials. Daria assumed that would sour anyone.

A familiar pull shot through the delicate veins of her tail. Another bolt of magic ran through the water, stronger this time. Her mother was calling her.

Daria made her way downstream to a bend in the creek. She pulled herself out of the water, onto dry land, and let the magic change her. Her tail separated and slimmed until two long legs appeared. Everything about her looked perfectly human, although her toes, like her fingers, were slightly webbed. No gills, no fins, no scales, except for a small patch of glittering red at the bottom of her spine.

Pulling on jeans, holey Chucks, and an old T-shirt that read "Thanks for all the fish" from the cache by the willow, she called her mom as soon as she got back to the house.

"Hey mama."

"He's free." Pelya Czernovitch minced no words, but there was a discernible tremble in her voice.

Daria froze. An icy cold that had nothing to do with swimming in January seeped through her, freezing her blood and bones. Peter Rollins, the man who had attacked her and changed the course of her life, must have been granted an early release.

Magic's Song

When most of her peers were in high school, Daria and her sisters, all *rusalkas* with gifted voices, had been on stages across the world. Their group, Sirenas, sang a blend of appealingly eerie Russian folk music and pop that captured an audience at exactly the right time. During one of their breaks back home in the small town of Volshev, Texas, Daria had been walking home from a friend's house when Rollins, a super-fan who attended all their concerts and even moved to their hometown, pulled up beside her.

Sometimes, she could still feel his cruel fingers digging into her arms as he dragged her toward his van, whispering in her ear about how he'd take such good care of her. All she had to do was sing for him. Just for him.

So she had. A wave of rage and hatred that she'd never felt in all of her seventeen years came over her, and she opened her mouth and sang, right there on the dim, little side street where he'd stopped her.

She sang a song of death, of cold so deep it froze the soul. She sang of icy rage and vengeance and bitter retribution.

Her voice finally broke, and she was coughing up blood from her torn throat when the police arrived. Rollins writhed at her feet, bleeding from his ears and nose, eyes rolled up in his head as he seized and spasmed. As the EMTs worked on him, he woke long enough to scream like demons were tearing the flesh from his body. He fell into a coma on the way to the hospital.

When he awoke three months later, the state placed him in a mental institution, trying to get him sane enough to stand trial. He'd been there for ten years.

Daria left Sirenas. It took weeks for her voice to recover, and when it did, she'd refused to sing. When school started the next fall, she left Texas far behind, changed her last name to Black, and earned degrees in Environmental Science and

Biochemistry to work on keeping waterways safe and protected. She was a water fae. Clean water was kind of a thing for her.

After all these years, and a good bit of therapy, she thought she'd left Rollins in her past.

"Has he hurt anyone?" she finally asked.

"No. There's a court order forbidding him from coming near us, or attending any concerts. But I'm worried, *ptitchka*."

"He can't find me, mama. How could he? I have a new name, I don't sing anymore, and I live in Georgia. I don't even have social media accounts he could track." Reciting the things that made her feel safe calmed her a little. She'd be fine.

"I don't know, little bird. I have a bad feeling."

Daria forced herself to sound positive. "Don't worry. I promise you, he can't get to me."

After doing the obligatory, affectionate check-in on the rest of the family, and listening to her mother complain about Rodion, Daria's only brother, she hung up and let the smile drop from her face. Her cheeks ached.

Dread swamped her, but she fought it back, using the calming techniques she'd learned in therapy.

She was safe. He couldn't get to her. Everything would be fine.

A text appeared on her phone. Carina Valdis, a friend of hers, was proposing a girl's night out at Howler's, a comfortable local bar run by a werewolf who also happened to be the sheriff's sister.

Less than an hour later, she slid into a small booth across from Carina and next to Katya Dostoyevna, another Russian with ties to Volshev, and the other member of their trio.

"So," she asked Carina once they were all settled in with their drinks. "What brought this on?"

"Men are stupid," Carina said.

Daria and Katya looked at each other. "Boyfriend troubles?" asked Katya, who was shy to the point of speechlessness around most people but had a secretly raunchy sense of humor with her friends.

"Not anymore. Turns out, the smell of paint gives him hives."

"Wow. Talk about a deal breaker." Daria commiserated. Carina was an artist, so that relationship would never have worked out. Sadly, none of her boyfriends seemed to last very long, no matter what. Allergies were a new one, though. This deserved a toast.

"Here's to better luck next time. *Za zdrovye*!" Daria and Katya had taught Carina the words. They clinked then drank. After a moment, Katya spoke up.

"I got another letter from him." The girl was too sweet for her own good, Daria knew, except when it came to her animals. Katya had been sent here by her family the day after she graduated from high school to care for an elderly aunt. Somewhere along the way, she had begun collecting supernatural strays, nursing them back to health, and getting them adopted by families in town. Eventually, she had established an official animal sanctuary, backed by the Ellinghams.

Now Katya was being called back home to fulfill an antiquated promise to marry one of Volshev's golden boys. The two had maintained a stiff and formal correspondence since she left Texas – a letter on their birthdays, one at Easter, and one at Christmas. But over the last year, he had written more frequently, and Katya told her friends she was afraid he was finally ready to fulfill his end of the promise, whether she liked it or not.

Between them, the girls decided that in her next letter, Katya needed to ask him straight-out what the deal was. At least then she'd know what she had to face. Problem temporarily solved, they toasted again.

"*Vashe zdrovye!*"

Finally, it was Daria's turn. "I don't know if men are so much stupid as they are weird. And frustrating."

"Here, here," said the other two as they clinked their wine glasses again.

She gave them an abbreviated version of the man she'd seen at the creek, and how he'd seen her, even after drinking the enchanted water.

Katya stopped her. "That's weird, but how is he frustrating?"

Daria felt her cheeks heat. It had been a while since anyone had sparked her interest, and she recalled the way her body had responded to him.

"Ooooh," said Katya with a grin, waggling her eyebrows at Carina. "That kind of frustrating."

The girls giggled and Daria couldn't help but join in. At least she'd finally had something to contribute to their nights out that wasn't about work.

When they calmed down, Carina asked, "So is he supernatural, or isn't he?"

"He was so surprised and shocked, he couldn't possibly be like us. He has to be human, which means the water isn't working." She sighed. "I really am going to have to call Alice. I'm just putting it off because she's not..."

"Pleasant? Easy?" supplied Carina.

"In possession of a shred of sympathy or humanity?" finished Katya.

"I'll take all of the above for six hundred. But that's not all." She took a deep breath, then filled them in on her mother's phone call. And everything that had gone before.

"We had no idea you'd gone through all this." Carina's eyes filled with tears while Katya's filled with fire.

"I would just like to see him try something here. I'll cook him alive!"

"Nobody's cooking anybody," Daria said, but she was glad she'd finally told her friends. Their support made her feel so much better after the beating her heart had taken today.

"But I wouldn't mind eating *him* up with a spoon." Katya, the one who stammered if a man so much as glanced her way, was looking carefully over Daria's shoulder. "Shh! Don't turn around!"

Daria had started to twist in her seat, then laughed at her friend. "Then how am I supposed to see him? Anyway, I thought we were off men."

"Only the ones giving us fits. Everyone else is fair game. And I saw him first."

Daria and Carina smiled, knowing their friend would sooner cut off her extraordinarily long hair than talk to a stranger.

Katya's eyes grew round. "He's coming over here. Gah!" She buried her face in her wine glass to hide.

"Ma'am, I'm sorry to bother you, but..."

Daria whirled to face the familiar voice. It was the man from the pond. He looked better now, warm and dry. His hair curled over his high brow, and there was a fire in those brown eyes she'd never imagined would be aimed at her.

"It really is you." He had a dimple. Just one, deep in his right cheek. It took a lot of willpower not to sigh a little. "I told Nick I must have imagined you."

Another man stepped up next to the table. Nick Hardwin was a fixture in town, almost literally. A deputy sheriff by day, he appeared as his gargoyle self in the evenings, keeping watch over the town center. The humans thought he was nothing more than a statue, but he stood guard over them all.

"Ladies." He greeted them politely, then introduced his friend. "This is Trick Scanlon, an old Army buddy of mine."

Her eyes were fixed on him, and she held out her hand automatically. "Daria Czer–" She stopped herself, shocked at her misstep. She hadn't introduced herself with her real name in almost ten years. She backpedaled. "Black. I'm Daria Black."

"And you're not a, y'know..."

"Definitely not a mermaid." Because she wasn't a mermaid, she was a *rusalka*. Hans Christian Anderson could kiss her flippers.

Chapter Two

Trick was now convinced that he'd been seeing things earlier because there she was, his mermaid, with two long, slim legs encased in tight, dark jeans.

After arriving at the B&B where he was staying and showering some warmth back into his body, he'd met up with Nick for a beer at Howler's. Nick's fiancée, Willa Iscove, would meet them there after she closed the jewelry shop she owned. Over a strong, dark stout – one of the local brews – Trick told his buddy about his ride in, on the bike and on the horse.

"I swear, I thought she was a mermaid. But then I started thinking. There's that place in Florida with the girls in mermaid costumes swimming around. Weeki Wachee something. And you told me Nocturne Falls was heavy on the tourist stuff. So that's what I saw, right? A girl in a costume for a tourist attraction."

Nick smiled weakly. "Yeah. That's right. Tourist attraction."

"She looked so real." He took another swallow of his beer and stared into the mirror above the bar. In the reflection, a woman turned just far enough he could see her profile. "She looks... right there."

He wasn't sure what propelled him off his bar stool and over to the booth where she sat with her friends, but he couldn't stop himself once he started walking.

Her hair was the color of the wine she was drinking, a dark, rich red, and the sound of her laughter as she toasted made him feel drunk.

"Daria Black. Definitely not a mermaid," she said, and her voice when she spoke to him started the same fizz in his blood. He took her hand in his when she offered it, and didn't want to let go.

"Pleased to meet y'all." He nodded to the other two women.

The blonde one spoke up. "Trick Scanlon? I know who you are. I've listened to your music."

Trick still got a little thrill when people said that to him. "Thank you. I appreciate that."

"What do you sing?" asked Daria.

The blonde goggled at her. "Have you been living under a rock, girl? He's a country star. Remember I made you listen to that song, *Halfway to Home with You*?"

That had been his first hit, written while he was active duty and missing home. It was still one of his personal favorites, though he'd never found that fictional woman he'd sung about, waiting for him to come home.

Daria's eyes widened. "I love that song! You have a wonderful voice. It's–" she cut herself off and looked at Nick. "It's almost magical."

The way she said it sounded significant. His buddy caught her inflection and his eyebrows went up. "That's not... I'm going to text Willa." Nick walked away from them as he pulled his phone out and started tapping at it.

Magic's Song

Trick watched his friend leave, then turned to the woman at his side. "What are y'all talking about?"

One of her friends interrupted, the one who hadn't said anything yet. "Do you think he's...?"

"Have you heard his music? He's got a gift. Whether it's mundane or not, I don't know."

"Hello, ladies. Standing right here." He waved a hand at them, and Daria caught it in hers. Her unexpected touch felt comfortable somehow. As if they weren't strangers at all. She looked into his eyes and smiled.

"You must be so confused right now. Everything's fine. I didn't realize it until just now, but it's possible you might be a little more than you think you are."

"I don't even begin to know what that means." He took her other hand and raised it to his lips. "I'm not sure I care."

She watched him with wide eyes, then blushed furiously. He opened his mouth to tell her how much he wanted to hear her sing again, but someone tapped him hard on the shoulder.

"Trick Scanlon? Is that you? Hey, you guys! It's Trick Scanlon."

The rude word he thought didn't pass his lips. Instead, he shifted to put Daria slightly behind him as he turned to meet his fan.

He felt her slip away from him, and, not for the first time recently, he regretted his fame – the other side of the gratitude he also felt. But he was hip deep in it now, so he put on a smile and dropped into character. The famous Trick Scanlon, Country Music Star.

He tried to keep an eye out for her as he shook hands, took selfies, and signed autographs. She and her girlfriends had retreated to a dim corner, away from the crowd gathering around him. It wasn't long before the fans started asking him to sing, turning it into a chant.

Music began its familiar hum in his veins like it always did before a concert. He might be tired, but singing for a crowd, no matter how big or small, was as much a part of him as his own skin and bones.

Nick was carrying his guitar when he came back in with his arm around a woman, slim and blonde with huge eyes. Trick could have sworn her ears were slightly pointed, but it had to be something about her haircut. She waved at him, and he waved back. That must be Willa, Nick's fiancée.

Once Trick had the guitar in his hands, it seemed like only moments before a space was cleared on the dais on the hardwood dance floor, near the dark, corner booth where Daria and her friends sat. The tall, wild-haired woman who owned the bar set him up with a bar stool, a microphone and an amp. He was ready. Across the small space, his eyes connected with Daria's.

He started off with his own song, and it was all too easy to picture pretty, red-haired Daria as the woman standing on the front porch, waiting for her soldier's return.

A few more songs followed. Some were from his albums, some were old and new classics, a little Johnny Cash, a little Garth Brooks, and the audience got a kick out of him yodeling on Eddie Arnold's "Cattle Call." But the more he sang, the easier it was to hear Daria humming and singing along.

Each note was like an angel's song falling on his ear, and he wanted to stop and listen to her forever. There was a little difference this time, no extra added fizz, although her sweet singing was still better than anything he'd heard in his life.

"All right folks, one more song. But I'll only do it on one condition. If that pretty lady over there comes to sing with me." He held out a hand to Daria. He didn't want to embarrass her, but he needed to feel her voice blending with his.

Slowly, with the urging of her friends and the audience, she slid out of the booth. When he reached out to her, the feel of her slender fingers in his made his heart skip a beat.

"I don't mean to embarrass you," he whispered, away from the microphone.

"I hope I don't embarrass *you*," she answered. "It's been years since I was on stage."

He knew it. She'd done this before, and he couldn't imagine why she wasn't singing to sold-out houses all the time. Then he caught himself. He was here, singing in a bar in a tiny town, hiding from his manager and his band because that life was tougher than he'd ever imagined it could be.

"You're going to be great. What would you like to sing?"

"I haven't listened to a lot of country music, but I think I remember one from not too long ago."

They settled on a hauntingly lovely duet, a little sad but deeply romantic. As he picked out the first notes on his guitar, his heart swelled. For the first time in a long time, he felt the magic rise with the music. This was what he'd been missing. Singing had become a job instead of a joy, but when Daria began to harmonize with him on the chorus of "Whiskey Lullaby" chills broke over his skin.

The world shrank to just the two of them as they sang the story of two ill-fated lovers. When the final notes of the lullaby ended, silence blanketed the room.

A tear glistened on Daria's cheek, and Trick reached out to wipe it away with his thumb. Her skin was soft, warm silk under his hand, and he stayed, cupping her chin as he lowered his lips to hers.

The kiss held as much magic as the song, and even when the audience finally began to clap, he barely heard them.

They drew away from each other slowly and the bubble around them burst. Daria turned and waved shyly to the audience. Then she gave him one last, long look before making her way back to her booth with her friends.

The impromptu concert broke up and Trick packed away his guitar with care.

"That was something else." Willa approached him with an arm around Nick's waist. "You have a wonderful gift, but that last song was..."

Trick nodded. "Yeah. She's amazing."

"Daria is terrific, and it's in her blood to sing like that. You, on the other hand. May I?" She reached out for his hand, and he let her take it, a little uncomfortably. He wasn't in the habit of holding hands with another man's girlfriend. Nick shifted a bit to block them from view.

Trick watched Willa as she closed her eyes. She squeezed his fingers as her other hand traveled to the pretty purple stone on a pendant around her neck.

Her eyes finally opened, and he was stunned to see that they glowed with an otherworldly light.

"Oh, you are a rare one." She smiled widely at him.

"Thank you? Nick?" He looked for reassurance from his friend. Also, did he know his girlfriend glowed?

"It's all good, Trick."

Trick closed his eyes and tried to breathe, to calm himself. This was one of those moments that changed things, he could feel it. His heart began to pound, and he grasped for the calming strategies one of the VA therapists had taught him a few years ago, but they weren't working this time.

The space he was in started to feel small. He blinked and the bar started to blur around the edges, changing to a small hut in Afghanistan. More of a lean-to propped up against a mountain. It hadn't looked like much until he walked in, shadows moving everywhere from the bitter wind that blew through open windows. It wasn't enough to clear away the heavy smell that assaulted his senses. Trick squeezed his eyes closed to shut out the memories of what...who...he'd seen lying on the floor of that lean-to. She was so small. She'd been so tiny.

He had to get out.

Small fingers slipped into his free hand. "Is everything all right?"

THE MAN who had kissed her as though they were alone on a desert island looked like he needed a friend.

Actually, he was sweating and pale and looked more like he needed an intervention, so that's what she did.

She said good-bye to her friends, then stepped past the gargoyle to get to Trick. The moment she wove her fingers through his, he opened his eyes. He caught her gaze as if that desert island they were on was covered in quicksand and she was the one with the rope.

Never breaking eye contact, she spoke to the side. "Nick, you need to step back. Both of you, move."

She heard Nick murmur something to Willa, and they both shifted away, widening the space around Trick.

"Let's get you out of here," she whispered to him, keeping her eyes on his, leading him to the rear exit.

"Hey Trick! You gonna sing for us anymore?" yelled out one of his fans.

He was still white-faced, and she whispered, "Just wave, Trick. That's all you have to do." He nodded and lifted an arm.

"He's done for the night, but thanks!" Daria called out to the fan cheerfully. Then she wrapped her hand around his waist and pulled his arm over her shoulder, knowing the strangers behind her would jump to the wrong conclusions – that they were heading out back to make out, or more. She didn't care what the tourists thought of her. There were more important things going on.

Trick was getting heavier and heavier, and she hoped they could make it outside before he became too much for her to hold.

From behind her, Nick's long arm stretched forward and opened the back door for them.

"Thanks," she gasped, then stumbled down the steps into the cold night, illuminated by nothing more than a single lamp.

Wrapped up in each other's arms, they sank down to the ground. Wordlessly, they held onto each other while he shivered as if he'd taken another ride through freezing waters.

Long minutes passed until his grip on her softened.

"You keep saving me." His voice, deep and a little rough, reached inside her and smoothed over the places that had been battered by life.

"I'm happy to help."

He rearranged his arm around her and pulled her close, warming her. Daria enjoyed the closeness, the heat of his body, the rhythm of his heart as its frantic thump evened out. She started to hum, a soothing lullaby her mother had sung to her when she was small and afraid. And, she remembered, her mother had sung the same tune after Rollins had attacked her. For months, out of nowhere, she would freeze and start to shake, the memory of his attack so clear in her mind it was as if he was standing in front of her again. But then her mother's song would come to her, and she'd be able to breathe again.

She didn't know what Trick had seen, and she wouldn't pry. If he wanted to tell her, he would. For now, all that mattered was getting him back to an even keel.

The words tumbled, indistinct, from her lips as she

pulled the siren's magic from within herself. The song became more than just music, it became a healing. The same way she'd used it earlier to calm the kelpie and help Trick recover from his impromptu swim, this magic reached inside him to soothe the harsh, painful memories.

As she sang, she became aware of another power rising up to meet hers. Another song, sung in counterpoint. It didn't interfere, but instead brought deeper notes to her simple melody. She'd never heard the music in anyone but her family, but she realized it came from Trick.

She should have recognized it when they sang together earlier, but she'd told herself it was just the chemistry between them.

This was more.

This was magic.

They sat and they sang to each other, the notes twining together to make something entirely new, sweet and strong.

Finally, the song faded away, but the weight holding both of them down had lightened.

A sniffle sounded in the darkness, and they scrambled to their feet. Trick stepped forward, one strong arm in front of her.

"I'm sorry," said Willa, stepping into the dim lamplight with Nick behind her. "We didn't mean to eavesdrop. We were coming to see if we could help, and bring you your things, but then..." She sniffed again, tears silver on her cheeks. "That was beautiful, Trick. *Rydych chi'n mab o Taliesin.*"

"Beg pardon?" He looked back at Daria, but she shrugged as she stepped up next to him. She'd never heard those words before.

"You are a Son of Taliesin."

He shook his head. "And that means..."

"You're a bard, Trick. Way back in the family tree, one of

your forefathers was Taliesin, the Welsh bard who chronicled King Arthur. He was given the gift of his voice and his song by the gods, and it passed down through his line. Bards were revered, and Druids thought that the gift of song was the highest magic one could be born with."

He raised his eyebrows. "Still not sure what that means."

Daria understood, though. "That's why he could see me. There's nothing wrong with the water."

"Looks like it." Nick nodded thoughtfully. "Explains how our unit has had a lot fewer problems transitioning to civilian life than so many others. Trick sang us through it."

Trick waved his hand. "Y'all suck at explaining things. Daria, do you know what they're talking about?"

"I do. I can explain it for you." She took a deep breath and gathered her courage. "Would you like to come over for a cup of coffee while we talk?"

There hadn't been a man in her house since she moved to Nocturne Falls, but this felt... important.

He smiled. "I'd love to."

They took their leave from Nick and Willa and she drove back to her house as Trick followed on his bike.

"Welcome," she said, opening the door and turning on the lights. She loved the little home she'd made after so many years in school, never settling down, trying to outrun her past. The walls were a cool, soothing blue that blended with the greens and grays she favored.

Water was everywhere. Paintings of oceans and rivers, bowls of multihued sea glass, small fountains and running water features in all corners of the room. Best of all, the long wall of the living area was taken up entirely with a massive fish tank.

"This is a really nice place," said Trick. He ran his hand through one of the bowls of sea glass in the entryway. "What are these?"

Daria smiled. "They're called mermaid's tears."

"I thought you said you weren't a mermaid."

"I'm not. I'm a *rusalka*. A Russian water fae, not some sad bit of sea foam from a fairy tale." He didn't respond, she so continued. "Come on," she said, taking his hand. "I'll get coffee going and see if I can explain it."

Chapter Three

Trick didn't drink, but he let the cup warm his fingers, and tried to understand what Daria was saying.

He was magic. Or something.

Some old dude in Wales had been King Arthur's court storyteller or official biographer or whatever, but he'd been given a magical gift of song and storytelling by the gods, and he passed that magic on to his offspring.

And that's why Trick literally had a magical voice. Just a trickle. Just enough to see magic in others and just enough that he could make people feel the songs he sang in a way that most other singers couldn't. His music touched people's hearts.

"That sounds really... useless."

Daria had settled next to him on the couch, close enough that their knees and elbows brushed occasionally. She'd been so patient with him, answering all his questions and listening to him ramble.

"What do you mean?"

"Well, unless you're a professional musician, what good

is a pretty voice? There are singers who are better than I am. Have nicer, clearer, more perfect voices."

"That's not all there is to this magic. You can change the way people feel with your songs. There's power in your voice. And that means, well, you know how it goes."

"With great power comes great responsibility?"

"Exactly." They grinned at each other, happy to share a nerd moment.

"Still not sure I quite get it."

Daria leaned over and put her cup on a coaster on the coffee table. "You don't know what a *rusalka* is, do you?"

"You said you were a Russian water fae. I saw a mermaid. Also, I've heard you sing."

"Well, we're not quite mermaids. We don't sing pretty songs while we comb our hair on a rock for fun. The fae world isn't like this one. It's dangerous, and we're one of the dangerous things in it." She moved away from him a little and looked over at the fish tank. "Our song is meant to lure the unwary. Just like that kelpie could have dragged you under the water until you drowned, I could have sung to you until all you wanted to do was walk into the water. You never would have thought about swimming away."

Trick considered his next move. The shame in her voice didn't sit right with him, but the image of her pulling him down into the water gave him the chills. He had a decision to make.

"Have you ever drowned anyone?"

She gasped. "I would never –"

"Then I'm not worried. Or scared of you, or disgusted, or whatever you think I'm supposed to be right now. Sugar, I was an Army Ranger. I've done a lot worse than you. If it comes down to it, there aren't many people in the world, magical or not, who are more dangerous than I am."

The sobbing laugh that burst out of her made him frown. "Oh, Trick. If only you knew what I've done."

He grasped her shoulders and turned her until he could see the tears streaming down her cheeks. He pulled her into his arms and held her as she cried. It was the least and the best he could do after she'd held him at the bar like she'd known how to handle his flashback. He didn't have them often, but he'd been glad to be among friends this time.

Finally, she wound down into little snuffles against his shoulder.

"I'm so sorry. We barely know each other and I'm blubbering all over you."

"I think we're more than even, sweetheart." He wasn't given to calling every woman he met sugar or sweetheart, but the words felt right in his mouth. "You want to tell me what happened? How you knew what to do back at Howler's? Because I've got a feeling those two stories go together."

She nodded, and he held her closer as the words tumbled out.

As she described her fear when Rollins had grabbed her, Trick felt his skin go hot. He wanted to crush that man under his boots. But Daria wasn't finished.

"Trick, the worst part was the song. It..."

"What, honey? What happened?"

"It felt good. As if there was something empty inside me and all that anger... I was so hungry."

All the heat of Trick's rage iced over. "Yeah. I know that feeling."

"I broke him. He was in a coma for three months. They had to send him to a mental institution. He's out now."

"He's what?" He grabbed her by the shoulders and pulled her back enough to look into her face. At the very real fear that pulled at her mouth and set little lines of tension around her eyes.

"I left you at the pond because my mother was calling me. There's a pull in the water, hard to explain..."

"Then I'll take it on faith. Daria, I believe you. I don't understand it all yet, but I believe you. Now, you were saying your mama called."

"That's what she needed to tell me. He's out. He's not allowed to approach anyone in my family, and so far, he hasn't. But I'm so worried about them."

"What about you? Aren't you worried about yourself?"

"I left town, changed my name, and went to school for something totally unrelated to music. I don't use any social media. He can't find me."

He dragged Daria onto his lap and squeezed her. "You gave up your whole life for that..." He said a lot of words that made her blush, but he was unrepentant. Rollins was every single one of those descriptors and then some.

By the time he wound down, she was giggling. "I'm pretty sure some of those terms don't go together."

"If they make you smile, then they go together just fine."

He settled back against the soft couch, comfortable with her in his arms.

"So that's why you knew what to do when I had a flashback. You get them, too."

She nodded, her fingers trailing aimlessly over his shirt. "They're not as bad as they were, but today was tough."

"Yeah, I can imagine."

They sat in silence for a while, and he enjoyed the quiet more than he'd ever thought he could. It was what he'd been craving. So much noise inside his head while he was running the hamster wheel of his career. Who'd have ever thought a side trip to a little town would make such a difference?

Soon, she was asleep.

A mermaid – no, a *rusalka* – was asleep on his lap. He was a magic man with magic in his arms.

Partway through the night, he half-opened his eyes and readjusted them so they were both lying down. With her back pulled tightly into his chest, his knees tucked under her bent ones, and his arm secure around her waist, it was the best night's sleep he'd had in months.

His phone woke him, weak winter sun filtering through the windows. He was alone, a fluffy ocean blue blanket draped over him. And was that fresh coffee he smelled?

He stared blearily at the little screen in his hand. A text from his manager, George Williams. Trick looked at the little flashing notification light, and it beeped again. Another text. Then another.

Can't buy this kind of publicity!
Where is this town?
People are loving it! It's trending on YouTube!

Trick went into the kitchen, poured two cups of coffee, and took a big swallow of his. He burned his tongue, but he needed the shot. He shook his head. That was some strong java.

What are you talking about? he texted back.
Haven't you seen this? Who is she?

George attached a video, a little bouncy and a bit blurred in places, and Trick watched it all. His heart stopped, then rushed to catch up. It was him and Daria, singing together.

They sounded amazing. The song was haunting and beautiful, and her pure voice lent it a sadness that twisted around inside his chest. Pure chart-hitting gold. Then he read down.

Daria wasn't tagged by name, but his gut rolled when one of the sharp-eyed commenters asked if she was that girl who used to sing with Sirenas. Crap. She was out there now where Rollins could find her.

This was his fault.

The object of his thoughts came strolling out of her bedroom, smelling sweet and fresh, looking put together and business-like in a silky blouse and sharp black trousers, pearls in her ears, and her hair pulled up neatly in a clip. She couldn't have looked more human.

Just like that, he believed in magic and mermaids and true love. Nothing else was important.

For a split second, he thought about proposing, but two things stopped him. First, he didn't have a ring. Second, he was pretty sure she'd scream and run away. But maybe not too loud or too far.

Because as she walked toward him, her gait shifted from upright professional to loose-hipped and sexy.

DARIA COULD DEFINITELY WAKE up happy in Trick's arms for the rest of her mornings. An hour ago, it had been a battle to convince herself she needed to slide slowly out of his sleeping embrace and get ready for work. Now, here he was, standing in her kitchen, rumpled and warm in his big socks and jeans that hung just right on his hipbones.

Best of all, he was holding out a cup of coffee.

She'd found the perfect man.

"Good morning, beautiful." His voice was a sexy, sleepy growl that sent all sorts of nerve endings tingling. If he proposed to her right that second, she'd have been tempted to say yes.

Instead, she murmured, "Mmmm, *spasibo*."

She reached for the coffee, but he pulled it away. She watched in dismay as the cup traveled out of her reach, but all of her thoughts were derailed when he took her into his arms instead.

"Does that mean thank you?" That rumbling voice did even more intimate damage up close, his breath on the sensitive spot under her ear.

"Mmmhmm," she said, winding her arms around his neck. "And so does this."

It was the sort of kiss that could have led to all sorts of interesting things if she hadn't had to go to work.

His phone beeped at him and he flinched, then reluctantly pulled back, letting his forehead rest against hers.

She sighed. If she wasn't going to get anymore kisses, she was really going to need that coffee.

With a final press of his lips against her hair, he let her go around the counter to pour sugar and a little cream into her cup.

"Would you like a little coffee to go with your sugar?"

"Oooh, original. I've never heard that one before." She grinned unrepentantly. So she liked her coffee light and sweet. Okay, really sweet.

But her smile faded when Trick's did. He stretched one arm over his chest to grab his opposite shoulder, and his fingers clenched over and over in an unconscious gesture, like a nervous tic.

"What's wrong?"

"I have some news, and I'm not sure how you're going to take it."

Daria put down the cup she'd just brought to her lips. Her fingers trembled as her mind ran wild.

He pulled his arm back to his side, took a deep breath, and blurted out, "There's video."

"Of what?" His words conjured up images that made her blush, even though they hadn't done anything.

"Us, singing last night."

She was still trying to catch up with what he was saying,

because a rush of unwarranted relief went through her. "Oh, is that all? That's..."

Oh.

Oh no.

"You weren't tagged, but someone in the comments recognized you." Her face must have shown her dismay because he walked over to her, and wrapped her in his arms. "I promise Rollins can't get to you."

She nodded into his shoulder. "Maybe he's not interested anymore. Maybe he doesn't care."

They stood for a minute, holding on to each other as tightly as they could. With a deep breath, they finally parted. Daria was proud that her hands didn't shake at all when she picked up her cooling cup of coffee.

"Everything will be fine," he said, and she agreed.

They lied to each other.

Daria couldn't concentrate on anything at work. Water quality was not holding her attention today. She was supposed to be doing drone work, inputting data she'd collected, but after the mistake that meant she had to start over for the fourth time, she stuck her head into her boss's office.

"Elizabeth, I'm not doing too well today. Mind if I head out?"

Her supervisor was a sweet older woman, entirely human, who didn't have a clue about the fact that half of her workforce were creatures from dreams and nightmares.

"Are you okay?"

She dredged up a fake smile. "Just... not feeling great. I've been trying to input that set of suspended sediment data and I keep screwing it up."

Elizabeth nodded. "Some days are like that. I don't think you've ever asked for time off like this, so it's fine. Go get some rest. Hope you feel better."

"Thanks, I appreciate it." Daria was out of the office minutes later.

She and Trick had parted ways when she left her house that morning. He'd said he was going back to the B&B to clean up, then meeting Nick for lunch at Mummy's Diner.

"I'll call you when you get off work. Let me buy you dinner," he'd said, rubbing his hands over her shoulders for comfort. His or hers, she didn't know.

She'd agreed gladly. It would be like a real date. Not that she was good date material right now.

Only one thing could make her feel better.

She changed out of her work outfit and into a swimsuit. Then she slipped into a robe and carried a change of clothes down to the willow. Dropping the robe and the bikini bottoms, she put her feet in the water and let the magic transform and carry her into the creek. She startled a sleepy trout, and the fish's panicky leap made her smile as it swam away.

Daria went upstream, letting the water wash over her and take her fear and anger with it. The further she swam, the better she felt. When she got to Nix's Pond, she heard a familiar voice.

Trick sat on the bank with his guitar, bundled up against the chill. A pad of music paper and a pencil lay on one side of him, a bag of apples on the other, and a black horse drooled chunks of apple onto the grass behind him.

He was singing a lullaby to the kelpie.

Something soft and sweet and familiar, though she didn't know the words. The black horse's ears were pointed forward, all its attention on Trick.

She must have made some sound, because he turned his attention to her, and she was trapped by the look in his eyes. One of tenderness, welcome, and an open heart.

Her fear and anxiety swept away by the slow, steady

current, she swam to him and leaned on a rock. He never stopped playing, but pushed the sheet music toward her with the toe of his boot, the lyrics printed in English and some other language.

Sleep, my baby on mama's shoulder
Nothing will ever do you harm
Sleep, my baby, sweetly dreaming
As you rest in mama's arms.

Together, they sang, lifting each other through the highs, harmonizing where they caught the right notes until finally, the song came to an end.

"Trick, that's beautiful. Did you write those lyrics?"

"I'm working on them. The original is in Welsh. I'm playing around with some of the translations." He put aside his guitar and crawled over to her, then leaned down until their faces were level. "I thought you'd still be at work. So tell me, sugar. How was your day?"

"*Kapriznyi*." She shrugged, trying to find the right word in English. "Sort of restless and jittery, so I left a little early. Being in the water helps." She pushed herself up on her arms to bring them close enough to kiss, a leisurely exploration of lips that left them both smiling and breathless.

"That helps, too. How about your day?" she asked. "What did you do aside from learn songs in Welsh?"

"Had lunch with Nick and Willa. Learned a little more about this *mab o Taliesin* thing." He reached down for her hands, and she let him pull her out of the water until she was seated on the overhanging rock with only the tip of her tail floating in the current.

"You are so pretty like that. The color matches your hair and you look like a fairy tale." He relaxed next to her, and the horse whickered at them.

"That's right. I don't know if y'all have met. This here is Bubba." His accent broadened to a comical country twang.

Daria burst out laughing. "Bubba? Bubba the Scottish Kelpie?"

The water horse nodded its head up and down and pawed at the dry grass. "That's right, Bubba. Bubba here likes apples, don't you, boy?" Trick tossed a fruit at the kelpie, who caught it in his strong teeth, then chomped down with relish.

"I could have sworn that when I first met you, it was right after *Bubba here* tried to drown you."

"We had a discussion about that, Bubba and I." Trick's eyes were alight with fun, and Daria couldn't help but join in. "I am now convinced that Bubba was simply delivering me to you. Making sure we got together. He doesn't want us to be lonely."

"Well, Bubba, that was very sweet and thoughtful of you. I'm sure I owe you sugar cubes for that."

The horse whickered at them, then decided he was needed elsewhere as he ambled back into the brush surrounding the creek.

"Maybe someone's calling him for dinner. And I believe I promised you dinner tonight, too."

"So you did. I'll head back to the house and meet you at the B&B."

He shook his head. "Nope. I may have gathered a lot of bad habits along the way, but my mama would pinch my head off for treating you poorly. I'm borrowing Nick's car, then coming to pick you up."

"That would be wonderful." Daria knew she was blushing, but his manners were so sweet and nice. "I'll see you in an hour, then."

With a final, lingering kiss, she slipped back into the water, her worries and troubles forgotten.

Chapter Four

Trick banged his hand against the wheel of his borrowed car.

That video – and his stupid idea of getting Daria to come on stage to begin with – was bringing nothing but grief. The comments had exploded. The moment someone mentioned Sirenas, the internet detectives had come out in force, so now everyone knew that it was Daria Czernovitch, "the sister who left the group," and, thanks to a mapping app, that the video was taken in Nocturne Falls, Georgia.

Even though she went by Daria Black now, it wouldn't be long before someone made that leap. She was hard to miss with that mass of wine-dark hair, and she was impossible to forget.

At least, she was to him.

He'd done this to her. Made her afraid. She'd tried to hide it when he saw her at the pond, but there was no missing the tension in her shoulders or the slight narrowing of her eyes. He'd known her for not quite a full day, and he could already see the change.

He'd told Nick about it, and Nick took him over to the

police station after lunch to talk to his boss, Hank Merrow, the sheriff of Nocturne Falls and their former commander in their Ranger unit. Unfortunately, until Rollins made a move, there wasn't much the police could do.

After getting the official word, they'd had an interesting, if brief and slightly stilted, conversation.

"So Nick tells me you're some kind of magic singer."

"Looks like it." Trick nodded.

"Very interesting. I'm a werewolf. So is my wife. And that nosy old lady who brought you back here, who is also my aunt."

"I can hear you," called the spry older lady who had bustled him and Nick into Hank's office.

Hank poked his temple like he was pushing back a headache.

Trick raised a brow. "She's a werewolf."

"Yep."

"Well...okay then."

Hank's phone rang, and he went back to being all business. "You have a good day now, Trick. Don't be a stranger."

He'd walked out of the station feeling like he'd been hit over the head with a brick.

Speaking of bricks, it turned out that Nick was a gargoyle. A stone gargoyle. Which sounded a little ridiculous because of course a gargoyle is stone, but... It had been a blow to discover that not only was there a vast world of people who weren't regular old humans, but they'd been standing right beside him for years.

At first, he'd been hurt. Why hadn't they told him? Didn't they think they could trust him? Then he realized that there were some things you could only share with people who were like you. Mentally, he took a deep breath and let go of any resentment toward his friends.

But if he ever got his hands – or his supposedly magic voice – on Rollins, he wasn't going to let go of anything.

Distracted, he pulled into Daria's driveway and got out of the car. He rang the doorbell and wiped his slightly sweaty palms on his jeans as he waited for her to answer.

She opened the door and he had to stop and stare.

A dark green dress wrapped around her, playing up her slender curves and making her green eyes sparkle. Her hair was half piled up on her head in complicated curls, but the rest trailed long down her back.

"Honey, if you sat on a rock and never sang a note, I'd still dive into deep water to get to you."

Daria laughed, a rippling scale of beautiful notes. "I'm sure there's a very sweet compliment in there. Thank you. Come on in."

She finished fastening the ankle strap on a pretty pair of green high heels, grabbed her purse, and was ready to go. Suddenly, he was rethinking.

"I have to say, I'd just as soon stay in tonight."

"If I had anything in the house that was ready to eat, I'd agree with you. But you promised me dinner out." She smiled widely.

"I'm beginning to regret saying that." He nibbled on her neck, and she tilted her head back to let him for a moment before she put her hands on his chest.

A movement outside the window, a car driving down the street, snagged his attention for no reason he could think of. With a quick frown, he planted a kiss on her soft, silky cheek.

"Is something wrong?"

"Not a thing." He pulled her fingers up and kissed their tips. "You ready?"

Trick hadn't been sure what to expect from a pleasantly

dark pub called the Poisoned Apple, but the food, the ambiance, and especially the company, were all excellent.

He put his knife and fork on his plate after finishing a steak cooked perfectly medium-rare.

Daria said her pan-seared trout on a bed of wild rice was delicious, as well. "I spend half my life in the water. What did you expect me to eat?" she said, smiling when he raised his eyebrows at her choice.

He'd been eating so much junk food on the road, this was a welcome change. Although nothing beat watching her as they talked a little bit about everything.

She had an agile, fascinating mind. He admitted she was smarter than he was. The woman had her master's degree in environmental science with some kind of water resource management specialty. Trick had squeaked past high school chemistry with a C. But she didn't come across as superior about her education, instead asking him about his experiences as a Ranger and a singer.

His description of playing the Grand Ole Opry made her lean forward, and he was man enough to feel flattered by her interest.

Out of the corner of his eye, he saw a young couple hanging back and whispering. He sighed.

"Do you mind?" He flicked his eyes over.

"Not at all. They love you, and no wonder. You're wonderfully talented, and your songs mean something to them." She leaned in and covered his hand with hers. "Honestly, Trick, it's fine."

He usually didn't mind signing autographs and talking to fans, but sometimes – okay, right this minute with this beautiful woman across from him – he just wanted to keep a moment, a memory, for himself.

Trick blew out a short breath, then made eye contact with

the couple and gave them a small smile. The woman made a quiet, squeaking sound as she approached... Daria.

"You're Daria Czernovitch," she gasped breathlessly.

Daria's eyes were as wide as the fan's, and she nodded. "Yes, but..."

"I've been a huge fan of Sirenas for a long time. Would you mind signing an autograph for me?"

Trick was nearly as stunned as Daria until the humor of it caught up with him. He grinned as Daria chatted with her briefly and signed a napkin with a slightly shaky hand after asking how to spell her name and making introductions.

"This is Trick Scanlon."

The woman looked a little puzzled, but asked him politely, "Do you sing?"

He wanted so badly to laugh, but he smiled and said, "A little. Sometimes. Nice to meet y'all."

After a few final words, lavish compliments about Daria's singing, and a hopeful question about whether Daria was returning to the music world, they left.

The silence in their wake was thoughtful as he looked at the woman across the table from him, absently running her fingers over the tines of her dessert fork. "First autograph in a while?"

She nodded, her eyes a little troubled.

"Worried about Rollins?"

Daria's front teeth worried at her lip. "I am. I worked hard at staying under the radar. I haven't sung in public in years, and since I changed my name, no one here connected me with Sirenas."

Guilt punched him again, but he wouldn't bring that feeling to the table tonight. Instead, he changed the subject.

"Have you ever considered going back? Recording? Touring?"

"Not really. I was so busy at school, working and trying to forget, that the music sort of... got lost along the way."

"Maybe you've found it again?" He laced his fingers through hers.

"Maybe. I'm not sure. I love to sing, but I love what I do now, too."

"I don't think you have to decide right now. It's nice that people remember you. Like you said, your songs mean something to them."

That brought the smile back to her face, and he had to stop himself from leaning over the table and kissing her. Instead, he squeezed her hand in his, just enough to feel her squeeze back.

They got their dessert to go, and he enjoyed the way her dress slid over her hips as he followed her to the door.

She caught him watching when she turned to ask him a question, and he winked, unrepentant.

He opened the car door to put the paper bag holding their tiramisu on the seat while they went for a little walk around town. But the sense of being watched raised the hair on the back of his neck. When he was active duty, they called it "situational awareness." Now that he was a civilian, though, he sometimes found himself almost paranoid about watching his surroundings, a sort of hypervigilance. The counselor he'd seen for a while called it a symptom of his PTSD.

This was different. While the chaos of finding out that he had magic in his voice should have upset him, he found that settling into that new knowledge was easier than he'd anticipated. It felt right. Plus, dinner and Daria had helped him relax more than he'd been able to in a long time.

No, this was an echo of that same creeping feeling he'd caught while he was at her house.

"Trick, is everything okay?"

He dredged up a smile. "Yeah, I'm good." But he tracked the make and model of the cars in the parking lot as he walked back to her on the sidewalk, then took her hand in his.

There was something out there, waiting. And he'd be damned if it was going to get to her.

DARIA WATCHED Trick as he watched everything else. Between the restaurant and the car, he had changed. His eyes were bright and hard, his mouth taut and grim. This was not the man who had kissed her wildly in her foyer, not the man who had charmed her at dinner. This was the soldier, tense and guarded.

Finally, she stopped. Immediately, he covered her, stepping close to her body until she moved with him into the space of a shop's darkened door.

"Trick, you need to tell me what's going on. This is not okay."

He dropped his forehead to hers, and she read the torment in his eyes. "I'm sorry, Daria, but I have this feeling crawling up my spine. Someone's watching."

She wanted to protest, to tell him that he was scaring her a little, but she knew how much he cared, so she didn't object.

"Do you have a picture of him?"

She dug through her purse and pulled out her phone. "I do. I keep it to show police just in case." She hated that she always kept a constant reminder of the reason her life changed. Daria held up the image and let Trick study it. She didn't look at it. She didn't need to.

There was nothing remarkable about Peter Rollins' face. He was an average looking man, a little on the tall side, thin, a bit stooped, brown hair, brown eyes. Nothing about him drew the eye.

Her hand shook, remembering the grip of his strong fingers on her arm.

Trick took her phone and dropped it into her open purse before he pulled her in for a hug.

"Come on, let's make a quick stop, then we'll go home."

She nodded, and a little thrill went through her when he said "home" like it was something they shared.

He was still vigilant when they stepped out of the nook, but the haunted look had left his eyes. They walked across the street to the town square where a statue stood on a pedestal in the middle of a fountain.

He stopped in front of the statue, which sat in the pose of The Thinker, but with gargoyle wings sprouting from his back. Trick took both her hands in his and, though he flicked his eyes to the statue, he spoke directly to her.

"Hey Nick. I know you probably can't talk, but I know you're listening. Look, we're fairly sure Rollins is here. We haven't seen him, but you know the feeling. He must have driven like a bat out of hell to get here so quickly. Anyway, I'm taking Daria home, but I wanted to let you know he's around."

Daria was caught by the oddness of the subterfuge. Yes, it would have looked weird for both of them to stand and talk to a hunk of rock, but it felt much stranger to look at a man as he talked to someone else.

When she glanced up at Nick, he winked at her. A small and subtle move that made her smile.

"Hey, that tiramisu is calling my name," she said. "Let's go."

They breathed easier on the short ride home, as if they'd come full circle to the teasing and laughing they'd started with that evening. The feeling lasted through dessert and coffee.

"I'll be right back," said Trick as they moved to the couch.

Daria put the dishes in the dishwasher and was kicking off her shoes when he came back in carrying a small duffel.

"What's that?"

"My gear. I'm staying here tonight."

Both her eyebrows went up. "Oh really?"

"Yes, really. On the couch." He dropped the bag and wrapped his big, warm hands around her shoulders. "Daria, I swear I'm not presuming anything, but I don't feel comfortable leaving you here alone."

Alone. Daria had been alone for years. Ever since she left Volshev, even with rare visits home, she'd been on her own. Pride had made her carry on without anyone to lean on, to help her through times when she was so scared and lonely she wanted to cry. But she was tired of her cold pride.

She dropped her head to his chest and struggled to keep her tears to herself. Trick pulled her close and held her while she brought herself under control. She'd cried on him last night and didn't intend to abuse the privilege. She might be a water fae, but that didn't mean she was a watering pot.

Finally, she pulled back and wiped away any tears that had escaped. "Thank you. That's very thoughtful."

"It's not thoughtful. I just can't deal with the idea of you in danger."

"You're a protector, Trick. A soldier. I don't expect that's gone away simply because you're not in the service anymore."

His voice dropped to a sexy growl as he backed her up to the couch. "Honey, trust me. I may protect those in need, but what I'm feeling for you isn't duty or instinct. I know we've only known each other a couple of days, but I guarantee that this is something real. Something I want to hang onto. Forever, if you'll let me."

Daria felt like she had dived into deep waters and the pressure was going to burst her lungs.

So much overwhelming emotion, so soon, for someone she'd just met. It wasn't that she didn't feel the same way, but that she did. It couldn't possibly be real. Not this quickly.

She pulled away. "I need...I need to think. To breathe. I need some space, Trick."

The look in his eyes nearly killed her. It took everything she had not to give in and go along only because it felt like he'd spilled his heartblood all over her hands.

"I need some time," she blurted.

Her soldier straightened, and though she knew he was hurting, he gave her the warmest smile he could. "I understand. I do. It's okay, Daria. You take whatever time you need, and if you don't feel the same way, it's all right. I'd rather you think about it and get to the right answer, even if it means it's not me, than you jump in and find out later it was a mistake."

If she didn't know it would cause more heartache, she'd have hugged him for those words.

She did reach up and kiss him on the cheek. "Thank you. Let me get some sheets and blankets, and I'll make up the couch."

"You don't have to do that. I've slept a lot rougher than your nice couch."

"Trick Scanlon, are you under the impression that I wasn't raised right? That I don't know how to be a good hostess?"

He grinned. "No, ma'am."

"Then you step back and let me do my job."

Between them, they made the couch into a comfortable bed. When it was done, she stood awkwardly holding a pillow until he took it out of her hands. He leaned down and kissed her on the cheek, just like she'd done to him, and said, "Scoot. Go to bed. Rest, think, whatever you need to do. I'll see you in the morning. Don't be concerned if you hear me walking around. I don't always sleep well."

She nodded and headed to her room. In her camisole and sleep shorts, she stared out the wide French doors that looked out onto her back yard. The property went down to a bend in Wolf Creek, and she stood and contemplated its occasional glimmer for a long time.

Was it love or only infatuation? Maybe it was too soon for love. Although, did these things really operate on a timeline? Relationships changed things. Was she ready for change? Being with a man like Trick, who spent half his year traveling the country doing concerts, would she be all right with that? If she went with him, her career would languish. If she stayed home and worked, how could their relationship flourish?

Her thoughts were a knot of eels she couldn't untangle. The only thing that could help her get her thinking straight was time in the water.

A few clouds skittered over the dim face of the moon as she quietly crept out the door and down to the creek.

She was only a few steps from the water when she felt those fingers on her arm.

Chapter Five

Trick must have been more exhausted than he thought because the thing that woke him up was the sound of neighing.

"Bubba? What the..." He fought his way out of the nightmare he'd been having and landed on the floor. "Daria!"

No answer. He ran to her room and burst through the door, not caring if he woke her up or she yelled at him. But she wasn't there to yell. Swear words poured out of him in ways they were never meant to be used as he charged out her back door. The black magic horse waited for him in the yard, shaking his head and prancing.

"Where'd she go, Bubba?"

Trick knew the risk and counted it worth the cost as he pulled himself up onto the kelpie's back. Sure enough, the beast's magic worked and he stuck on like a burr.

He wasn't armed. Since he got out, he'd left his service weapon locked in a gun safe, where he took it out once a year to clean it. He told himself that one day he'd take up target shooting or something, but that day hadn't come yet.

He hoped he wouldn't need a firearm to deal with this. On the other hand, he hadn't spent all those years as a Ranger for nothing. He could do a lot more than pull a trigger.

Also, he was riding a devil horse, he had a magic voice, and he was on his way to rescue a merm– *rusalka*. Daria hated when people got those two things mixed up. She had abilities of her own. And if they were down by the water, she stood a better-than-even chance of coming away unharmed.

If... He didn't like qualifiers.

Bubba had been galloping along the side of the creek, and Trick's heart sank as he realized how far they'd come. How long had he been out?

Finally, the kelpie slowed and stopped, his flanks heaving, ears pointing forward.

"All right, boy. You gonna let me off?" he whispered, and one ear flicked back at him.

A shudder ran over the animal, and Trick, suddenly released from his imprisonment, barely caught himself before he slid to the ground. "Good boy, Bubba. You're gonna be up to your scary teeth in apples for life, I promise."

A man's voice filtered through the brush.

"I told you. I told you and told you and told you, my sweet Daria. You're only supposed to sing for me. And now I see that you're singing for all these other people? That you're singing with that man?"

He heard a rattle and a feminine gasp, a small sound of pain, and Trick was glad he didn't have a gun. He wanted to beat this guy to a pulp with his fists.

"Peter, you shouldn't be here." Her voice was rough and hoarse – there was no way she could sing with her throat so raw – but she tried to reason with the man. "You shouldn't have come here and taken me."

"If I hadn't, what would happen to you? You'd go on

singing, flaunting yourself on stage like some prostitute." He spat the word at her, and Trick decided to punch him one extra time just for that. Daria Black – or Czernovitch, or whatever she wanted to call herself – was the kindest, smartest woman he'd ever met. And if this nutbar called his woman a prostitute one more time, he was gonna lose teeth over it.

"I came to protect you," said Rollins.

"This isn't protecting me, Peter. You're hurting me." She coughed harshly.

"Only because you're being stubborn. If you'd stop fighting, I wouldn't have to do this. I wouldn't have to tie you up and hurt you."

Trick examined the terrain. His options sucked. Dry leaves all through the brush made it an impossible path for stealth. Going around it would take him too far out of the way before he could circle back, and then he wouldn't have enough cover to approach unseen.

The creek offered the only other option.

It would be colder than a well-digger's butt in Alaska, and if he stayed in it too long, he risked hypothermia. After his recent dunking, he wasn't eager to revisit that. But it was the only way to get to Daria quietly, without being seen.

He crawled into the creek, and it took all his willpower not to yell at the shock and pain of the icy water running over his skin. Behind him, Bubba stepped into the stream, as well, and whatever magic the horse had made him as silent as a ghost.

They only had to travel a few yards before they passed the brushline.

Daria was tied hand and foot, and propped up against a tree. She wasn't far from the creek, and Trick wondered why she hadn't just rolled down to the water. Then she twisted a little and the weak lantern that Rollins had set out illuminated a glimmer of metal around her throat.

She was wearing a collar. And not a strip of leather. She was wearing a pinch collar meant for a dog – metal prongs lined her neck – and Rollins was yanking the leash like he had a seizure disorder.

Tiny lines of blood dripped down her throat, and with her hands tied behind her back, she couldn't protect herself from his pulls.

This guy was going back to the hospital. In pieces.

He crawled through the shadows cast on the water until he was past her. His dark hair helped camouflage him as he moved. The cold, however, was an enemy as dangerous as Peter Rollins. He was beginning to shiver in deep, wracking shudders.

Trick climbed stealthily up onto the rocks that lined the edge of the creek but were below Rollins' line of sight from the bank.

"Why don't you sing for me now, Daria?"

She coughed in response, and it hurt Trick to listen to the harsh, painful sound.

Rollins paced around the lantern, muttering to himself and occasionally yanking the leash, so Trick took a chance. While Rollins was off on a delusional rant, Trick flicked water at Daria to catch her attention. She started and tried to turn her head to see him, but the movement brought Rollins' attention back to her.

"What? What's out there? Do you see him?" He looked around wildly.

Daria's head was bent and her shoulders shook with silent tears. Trick's heart ached as she drew Rollins closer.

"I told you he wouldn't come. He was using you. I'm the only one who can keep you safe, sweet Daria," he crooned to her.

She didn't answer, and Rollins gave the leash a vicious tug. Daria choked and coughed, deep, hacking sounds. One more yank like that and Rollins would crush her throat. Trick had to act now.

He was bigger and stronger than Rollins, but he didn't know if he was faster. It didn't matter, though, because all he had to do was get him to let go of that leash, and he'd take care of the rest from there.

Trick tensed his muscles to jump, but before he could move, a massive black shadow leapt over him.

Bubba, who had been silently watching from the watery shadows, sailed over the bank to land securely in front of Rollins. The man jumped back with a screech. The leash had been looped over his wrist, but he let it slide off in his haste to get away from the black demon beast.

Trick ran to Daria and gently pried the metal teeth of the collar from her neck where a couple of them had embedded themselves in her skin. The wickedly sharp pocket-knife he carried sliced away the zip ties around her wrists and ankles.

The moment her hands were free, she reached for her throat, still coughing. He tried to take her in his arms, but she pushed away, leaning toward the creek, crawling for it.

"The water? You need to be in the water?"

She nodded weakly, her eyelids fluttering. Rollins had hurt her badly, maybe crushed her throat with his last ferocious yank. She was a *rusalka*. Maybe the water could heal her. Trick grabbed her up and took a running leap toward the water, both of them landing in it together.

Trick thought he knew what magic felt like. He felt it when he rode the black kelpie and when he sang with Daria. He felt it when they kissed. But holding her in his arms as she shifted from human woman to beautiful, haunting fae creature was beyond anything else he knew he'd ever experience. The water sparkled around them in a whirlpool of effervescent bubbles that popped and fizzed against his skin.

The robe she'd been wearing dissolved and gorgeous red and white scales flowed down from her waist, covering her long legs down to her toes, which disappeared to become translucent, delicate fins.

She thrashed, her wine red hair floating around her, winding around his body, tying them together. He was in over his head, unable to breathe, but he didn't care. He held magic in his arms and he wasn't letting go.

Daria's eyes shot open and she smiled. If that was his last sight on earth, Trick was dying a happy man.

Then things changed. He wasn't holding her anymore, she was holding him. Stronger than he'd thought possible, she looped her arms around his chest and pushed upward, to the night sky, to the free air.

HE'D COME FOR HER.

Trick had come for her when she was in her most desperate hour of need. She'd been on her way down to the water to think about him, about their relationship, about what she'd done with her life and where she was going.

Daria wondered if she wasn't still making Rollins more powerful than he was. Fear of him had dictated her life for so long that it was a curious shift to begin thinking of him as nothing more than the monster in her childhood closet.

Except, of course, there really had been a monster in her closet back then. Daria smiled at the memory. Her family's *domovoi* seemed to prefer her orderly closet and kept his bed there when he'd finished his household chores.

She'd been ready to dive into the water when Rollins captured her.

A blow to the head had disoriented her, giving the evil man time to slip that cursed collar around her throat. When she'd finally recovered enough to try to scream, the pain when he yanked on it took away her breath.

He'd dragged her through the brush, far down the creek. Every time she fell, barbed prickles had worked their way into the bare skin of her legs. He said he was taking her to his van, then they were going to drive away to their new home where no one would ever find them. Fear had flooded Daria in swamping waves.

When they'd reached this clearing, she stumbled and fell, choking against the constant, vicious tug of that hateful leash. He'd tried to soothe her.

"There, there now, my sweet. I know I'm being a little hard on you, but you... you made me so mad." He'd tried to explain himself to her, to rationalize his actions, but there was no excusing him. By putting her in the collar, he'd taken away her best weapon. "We'll rest a minute here before we keep going. I had to park quite a way off so that man wouldn't see me. He's already spotted me a couple of times today."

So Trick hadn't been paranoid and hypervigilant. She regretted ever doubting him. She regretted a lot of things. She regretted not answering when he'd said he wanted to hold onto her forever. His love was nothing like this agonizing, terrorizing obsession. And right now, she *really* regretted making up that bed for him on the couch. If they'd stayed together, she wouldn't have burrs embedded in her knees or a metal collar around her neck.

Then, like a miracle, he'd risen from her waters and rescued her. While Bubba charged Rollins, Trick had leapt into the water with her and saved her life. The shift from human to *rusalka* repaired her damaged throat and revived her. But Trick, for all that he could sing the birds down from the trees, was now in as much danger of dying from asphyxia as she had been a few moments earlier.

She dragged him up from the depths of the pond and pulled him over to the rocks, helping him crawl up onto dry land.

In the clearing, Bubba had continued to challenge Rollins, stamping his feet, charging, and snapping at him. The kelpie's eyes glowed red from within. The man kept trying to get away, but the horse was backing him into thick brush.

Daria huddled with Trick, trying to keep him warm as they watched the vicious dance. Finally, the Unseelie water horse got Rollins where he wanted him. Rollins put his hands out to keep his balance and touched Bubba.

The kelpie neighed in triumph as he dragged the man around the clearing, making sure he was never able to get his feet under him as he was pulled by one arm down the creek.

"Daria! Daria, help me!"

She searched her heart for kindness but found none. She was *rusalka*, not some sweet little water nymph, and not some weak fairy tale. Justice was her right and vengeance her heritage.

She spoke to the kelpie. "You know Sheriff Merrow's house? It backs to the water."

Bubba nodded his head, snapping at Rollins as he tried to get his feet under him.

"Try to make sure he's still alive when you get him there."

The magic stallion reared, a king of his kind, the embodiment of death and terror. Rollins screamed as the kelpie leapt for the water and dove under.

When the echo of his fear faded, Daria looked at Trick.

"Do you think I did the right thing? Should I have helped him?"

"Man put you in a dog collar and called you a prostitute. He's safer with Bubba than he would have been with me." Trick's cold voice comforted her.

She nodded. Rollins would wait until tomorrow – much later tomorrow. Right now, she wanted to go home.

Trick had warmed enough that only occasional shudders shook him, but his fingers were still icy when he put them on her chin. She let him move her as he examined her neck. "You all right, sweetheart?"

"I'm fine. Honestly, Trick. I'm okay. No lasting damage done." The water had healed her, as it always did. A little ache lingered, though. She'd been badly injured, but telling Trick now would only upset him.

"He still hurt you. And I still want to hurt him." His fists clenched, but he relaxed them to stroke her cheek.

"Well, I'm not wishing him peace and joy, but I don't want you to do anything you'd regret."

"I'm pretty sure I wouldn't regret beating him to a pulp."

She chuckled. "Maybe not, but I'd regret it when they arrested you for assault. Even if everyone agreed with you."

"Fine," he grumbled. "It's freezing out here. I thought Georgia was supposed to be warm."

"Georgia in January is cold. Come into the water. I'll keep you warm while I swim you home."

"You can do that?"

"I'm a *rusalka*. I can do anything I want in the water."

Trick grabbed her waist and pulled her close until she was sitting on his lap, her tail laying over his legs. "That's right. I've caught myself a beautiful Russian merm–"

"*Rusalka.*"

"Right. A beautiful Russian *rusalka*. And I do believe I'm in love."

"Will you write a song about this love?" She could tease now. She was able to sit in his lap, with her tail out for him to see, and laugh because he was so right for her.

"Absolutely. And it'll hit all the charts because everyone will feel the same way when they hear it."

Chapter Six

And they lived...

Five months later

"A Fish Woman Fell in Love with Me." Trick pulled Daria's hand up to his mouth and kissed the back of it.

"Nope," she said, smiling at him.

"My Gal's Just a Sad Bit of Sea Foam."

"Oh wow, that's almost good, yet somehow totally not." She actually snorted when she laughed at that one, so he knew she thought it was funny.

"How That Fairy Tale Guy Got Absolutely Everything Wrong."

"Yeah... no. Seriously, Trick, when are you going to tell me the title of the album?"

They were walking along the banks of Wolf Creek, enjoying the warmth of a sunny Georgia spring day. Trick's concert tour was over, and he didn't have another long stretch of travel scheduled until the next year. In the meantime, he'd told his manager that he'd be staying home, writing new songs, spending time in the studio, and reconnecting with the people he loved.

Technology was great. He'd set himself up with a small recording studio, and he could do nearly everything he needed to do with only monthly trips to meet with his Nashville producer. That meant he could spend most of his time with Daria.

He was living the dream.

Rollins was back in prison for life, or as good as. He'd been deemed mentally incompetent to stand trial until he was cured of his psychosis. At that point, he'd be tried and sentenced to a good, long stretch in the Georgia State Penitentiary. In the meantime, he was locked up in a mental institution because he kept babbling about a hell-horse that tried to drown him before werewolves had tried to eat him.

Somehow, the man had dislocated nearly every bone in his hand trying to get off Bubba before the kelpie shook him off at the sheriff's house. The off-duty sheriff and Alpha of his pack had been getting in some play-time with his mate and cubs *au naturel*, as it were, when Bubba and Rollins arrived. Hank had told the story in his quiet, solemn way, but the amused twinkle in his eye let everyone know he'd enjoyed that particular arrest quite a bit.

True to his promise, Trick never went down to the creek without an apple in his pocket. So far, the horse had a decided preference for big, sweet Honeycrisps, but turned up his nose at Red Delicious. As a joke, Trick had also brought sheets of dried nori once – Japanese seaweed used for making sushi – and Bubba crunched those up like they were candy. He'd had to make a line item in his budget for "horse treats."

Today, the kelpie meandered around them, occasionally tearing up a mouthful of sweet new grass.

"I'll tell you what, sugar. I'll answer your question if you answer mine."

They had reached Nix's Pond, where they'd first met that bitter winter eve. After such a tumultuous beginning, they'd agreed to take their time getting to know each other. Now Trick was done waiting.

After five months of being together as often as they could possibly manage it, he figured that they knew everything important about each other. She stole the covers and used his calves as foot warmers for her icy toes. She made coffee that should be considered a biological weapon. She spoke to her fish, and they answered back. She invested carefully and spent cautiously. She went out a couple of nights a month out with her friends, and if she'd had more than a single glass of wine, she was exuberantly affectionate when he picked her up.

Daria knew that he still had nightmares, and she was great about helping him out of tense situations without calling attention to it or showing him even a hint of pity. Her own nightmares were getting less and less frequent. She'd helped him design his new, little studio out behind her garage, and made it pretty and comfortable when he would have been satisfied with a chair and a bare light bulb. She missed him while he was gone, and when his tour was over, she'd welcomed him home with a small party of their friends. Then she'd sent everyone home and given him the welcome he really wanted.

Trick had met her family. A bunch of terrifyingly beautiful women, and when her mother greeted him, he'd never believed so hard that a *rusalka* could lure a man to his death just by singing at him.

Daria's father and brother were there, too. Her dad was

Magic's Song

almost normal. A quiet man who liked to do crosswords, he seemed to be the only one who could settle family squabbles. With only a few words, whoever was involved would murmur, "Yes, Papa," and that would be it. Magic.

Her brother, on the other hand, was a brooder. Rodion Czernovitch was the only son, and all the women doted on him, which seemed to make him impatient. By the second day of the visit, he'd come downstairs with his duffel still packed and claimed a "work emergency." After he kissed Daria, he'd pulled Trick in for a stiff bro-hug and whispered threats of bodily harm if his sister ever got so much as a paper cut on his watch, then took off like his heels were on fire.

Smart man. Trick liked him.

He and Daria walked this trail enough that they'd learned to stash a sturdy blanket in a chest hidden beneath one of the trees. He laid it out, but before she could sit down, he stopped her.

Trick took one of her hands in his and went down on one knee. His fingers were shaking so badly he could barely pull the little box out of his pocket.

He had given Willa his dog tags when he asked her to make the ring for him. She'd told him he needed to bring something of himself so she could weave the love and devotion into the jewelry. When he'd picked it up, even he had been able to feel the little thrill of magic in the Art Deco inspired, platinum filigree band with the square-cut sapphire. Not that he knew what most of those words meant, but Willa had seemed happy about it, so he learned them.

The look of shock on Daria's face made everything worthwhile. *She* made everything worthwhile. All the pain and hard work of getting to this point, where he'd try to be worthy of her, was the best part of his life.

"Daria Czernovitch, I know we said we'd spend time

getting to know each other, but my heart knows everything it needs to know. I love you, and I want to spend the rest of my life loving you. Will you be my wife?"

Her joyful acceptance ended up with them skinny dipping in the pond an hour or so later to cool off. She was doing lazy laps around him, her tail flicking droplets of water that glimmered like diamonds as he floated on his back, when suddenly she stopped.

"I answered your question. Now answer mine – what's the title of the new album?"

He grinned.

"Happy Ever After, sweetheart. I'm calling it...

Happy Ever After

Final Note

One final note:

This is the book that brought me back to country music. I grew up with it - my dad was a big Hank Williams and Patsy Cline fan - but once I hit high school, it was all Wham! and Madonna and INXS. Shut up. It was the 80s.

I started listening again when country went more mainstream in the 90s, and found that I really enjoyed Garth Brooks, Randy Travis, and Alan Jackson, but I listened to everything back then.

Cue marriage to a man who owns every Pink Floyd album. All of them.

Now imagine me singing "Stand By Your Man" in my head every time "The Wall" comes on.

I have Pandora stations of Latin pop, Celtic fusion, Disney tunes, and neo Punk (because some days you need a little My Chemical Romance). I feel like I have a pretty wide range of tastes in music, but I'm so glad I've added country back to the list.

I do mention a few specific songs in this book, made up

Final Note

at least one title - although if anyone writes "Halfway to Home with You," I'm going to be super impressed - and was also inspired by a Russian folk/pop singer named Pelegaya when the idea for Sirenas came into my head. I don't know if the group will appear in future books, but I loved the music I found. So here, for probably the first and last time in any of my books, is part of the playlist I listened to as I wrote.

Pelegaya: Пташечка (*Little Bird*)
Pelegaya: Ой, да не вечер (*Oh, Not Evening*)
James Rainbird and the Ambrosian Junior Choir: *Suo Gan* (Traditional Welsh lullaby)
Alison Krausse and Yo-Yo Ma: *Simple Gifts*
Brad Paisley and Alison Krausse: *Whiskey Lullaby*
Eddy Arnold and Leeann Rimes: *Cattle Call*
Garth Brooks: *The River*
Garth Brooks: *If Tomorrow Never Comes*
Johnny Cash: *I Walk the Line*
Johnny Cash: *Ring of Fire*
Randy Travis: *Diggin' Up Bones*
Alan Jackson: *Neon Rainbow*
Chris LeDoux: *Western Skies*
Dolly Parton: *Jolene*
George Strait: *Amarillo by Morning*
Tim McGraw: *Humble and Kind*

Magic's Fate

Chapter One

Rodion Czernovitch glared at his physical therapist. It wasn't Steve's fault that Rodion could barely make a fist with his right hand. No, the blame for that went to an enemy he'd left dead on the field of battle.

Still, the man in front of him was currently causing him a lot more pain than he'd ever admit, so he glared. And sweated. And squeezed that stupid ball until he imagined its stuffing spewing out all over the room.

When he looked down at it, however, his fingers were making a claw over the rubbery squeeze ball, but barely denting its surface.

He let go with a curse.

Steve, a mild-mannered, bald man with distinctly elfin features when he wasn't wearing his glamour, narrowed his eyes at Rodion, and said, "I think we're done for today."

Rodion tried to hide a sigh of relief. "Are you sure? Is our time over already?"

"No, it's not. I know Dr. Martinez sent you to me, but if you're not going to do the exercises on days you're not here, then I'm not sure why you keep showing up and wasting my time."

Rodion flushed with anger. He'd done the exercises diligently. "They don't help. Nothing helps. Shouldn't there be some improvement by now?"

"There is some improvement. When you got here, you could barely lift your arm, much less bend your fingers. Now you can at least keep the ball from falling out of your hand. And how are the muscle spasms?"

"Better," he admitted after a moment. "But it's still not enough."

"You're lucky you still have the arm at all. I'd say this is pretty good work."

"It's been almost four months since your original injury. I get that you want to go back to work, but you have to take the progress as it comes."

But what if it doesn't come? He didn't say it out loud, just nodded to Steve and promised to do more of the exercises on his own.

There was something wrong. He could feel it. He'd listened and asked questions and watched the doctor's faces during all his exams. He should be better by now and everyone knew it.

Late at night, he could feel the wound still inside him, deep down in the bone and marrow, where it refused to heal. Something wasn't right.

He wandered through the quiet streets of the quaint little tourist town where he now resided. Nice as it was, this wasn't his home. Home was back in Volshev, Texas, where his family – his hovering, smothering mother and six of his seven sisters – lived. Which is exactly why he was here in Nocturne Falls, Georgia, instead. He'd had to get away before he said or did something to hurt them when he knew they were only trying to help.

Magic's Fate

This was his compromise. The seventh sister, Daria, soon to be married to country music singer Trick Scanlon, lived and worked here. It comforted his mother that at least one member of his family would be able to take care of him.

Within two days of his arrival, Rodion and Daria had worked out an agreement where they had dinner once a week to check in, they were free to call on each other at any time, day or night, but they let each other live their own lives.

It was a perfect arrangement. Rodion had support when he needed help. His mother was mollified. And Daria, who had left Volshev years ago to get away from a stalker, had missed having family around. Rodion was enough of a connection that she was content, and he was happy to be there for her. But he'd had too much of family, and narrowing it down to Daria, who had never been a hoverer, was just enough of a link to keep the rest of them off his back while he recovered.

For now, he simply strolled down the streets of town, enjoying the peace and quiet. Later in the day, there would be people all over, coming to see the place where it was "Halloween – 365 Days a Year!" just like the welcome sign announced.

Rodion had always been an early riser. He was Steve's first patient of the day, which gave him the rest of the day to do... nothing. Back in Volshev, he would be getting ready for work. A quick workout and shower, breakfast, then putting on the uniform of the Border Crossing Patrol.

Keeping the minions of Koschei the Deathless on the Rus side of the fae/human border was full-time, dangerous work. It wasn't only the powerful, crazed fae lord who wanted to cross over and wreak death and destruction on the mortal world. There were always criminals of the more mundane kind of fae who tried to cross over with the refugees fleeing Koschei's reign. A pipeline funneling drugs tailored for the paranormal community had opened up in Volshev, and the BCP hadn't found the source yet.

Or at least they hadn't when Rodion had been injured and put on leave until he recovered.

If he recovered.

He shook off the negative thought and opened the door to the Hallowed Bean Coffee Shop. A few regulars nodded at him, and he nodded back, content with the continuation of their unspoken "I acknowledge your existence, but have no need to verbally interact with you" contract.

There was Pandora Williams with her fiancé, Cole Van Zant. Rodion had gone to their housewarming party soon after he arrived in Nocturne Falls, and Cole had proposed that night to Pandora in front of half the town. The man had courage.

At the next table, sat the massive dragon shifter and former MMA fighter, Ivan Tsvetkov, with his red-haired girlfriend, Monalisa Devlin. Ivan caught his eye and gave him a slight nod, which he returned. The giant Russian hadn't come through the border at Volshev, but he had stopped by the town and visited his many fans there a couple of times.

Rodion had talked with the man – not at the coffee shop – a few times since coming to town. It was always nice to use his native language, although Ivan was working to perfect his English. They weren't what he'd call buddies, but he genuinely liked the big bald guy.

The sheriff, a werewolf named Hank Merrow, was standing in line to order with his arm around his wife. As they stood, they chatted with one of the deputies, a Hispanic man who moved like a big cat.

Out of the corner of his eye, he caught sight of bright blonde hair with tendrils of rainbow color peeking through the curls. Carina Valdis, one of Daria's best friends.

Magic's Fate

He got in line and watched the pretty blonde woman discreetly. With her tablet propped up in front of her, she blew full, pursed lips over her cup of coffee, disturbing the rising steam as she read the screen. *Pretty* seemed a pale word to describe her. Talented, animated, intelligent, friendly – all applicable, but none of them were enough. *Sexy* worked, though, with that beautiful mouth, jade green eyes, and killer figure.

Also, *off limits*.

Daria would kill him if he got involved with her friend and they ended up not working out. And after she'd killed him, she'd hand his corpse over to the rest of his sisters and there wouldn't be enough left of him to bury in anything bigger than a teacup.

And if that wasn't enough, he had enough respect for the sexy artist to know that she deserved a man who was whole. So he was going to stay far away from Carina Valdis, no matter how much she appealed to him.

Large De-cappuccino – his usual plain cappuccino, served without a head – in hand, he sat down at the only empty table left, which was next to hers. She brightened when she saw him, and waved, but followed the shop's unspoken rule. Rodion nodded back and opened the copy of the *Tombstone* that had been left by the previous occupant of the table.

The paper straightened out before him, he absently reached for his coffee cup with his right hand.

At least, he tried to. He'd regained most of his large motor function after the injury, but he must have worked his muscles a little too hard this morning and his arm spasmed hard. All he managed to do was knock the cup onto its side, spilling the contents all over the paper and the table.

Fury and humiliation swept through him in waves of hot and cold.

The injury hadn't only taken the use of his arm, it had damaged his ability to control his magic. His father was a sorcerer – a *charodey* – like him, and his mother and all his sisters were *rusalki* – Russian water fae like mermaids, although they really hated being called mermaids. A few months ago, he could have controlled the spill with a thought, but now coffee dripped disconsolately off the edge of the table, making a creamy brown puddle on the tile floor.

Rodion wanted to stand up and scream. He wanted to up-end the table and send it crashing against the wall. But he wouldn't, couldn't lose his grip on himself like that. Before the accident, justified violence was part of his job. Now, however, he frequently felt like all his control was slipping away through his crabbed fingers.

A warm touch on his arm shocked him out of his rising temper.

"Rodion? It's all right."

He looked up into Carina's eyes, and pulled himself together. He nodded curtly and jerked his arm away. He didn't deserve the comfort of her hand if he couldn't keep hold of his own emotions.

She blinked, then any concern he might have read in her eyes was gone, hidden under the fringe of her hair and behind a bright smile. Carina grabbed a roll of paper towels, and started wiping up the liquid, talking as if he hadn't just been a huge jerk.

"How was therapy this morning?"

He grunted, ignoring the other people in the shop, and tried to help. He pulled the heavy trashcan closer, then balled up the wet newspaper and tossed it in.

"Looks like you're making progress."

Rodion glared at her. It was out of character for her to make a joke at anyone's expense.

"I mean that you're doing a much better job moving your

Magic's Fate

arm. When you got here, you couldn't have lifted it at all. This is progress." The honesty in her tone took away any lingering sting.

"Still can't move my fingers," he muttered.

Carina finished wiping up the last of the coffee, then handed him a clean paper towel. "For your shirt. And I'm sure you'll get there. You don't seem like the type to give up."

With another smile she excused herself to wash up, leaving quiet in her wake.

He was done here. There was only so much humiliation he was willing to take in one morning. He made another drink order to go and was waiting by the door when Carina caught up with him, a giant, colorful woven tote bag slung over her shoulder.

"Walking home?" she asked, fishing around in the bag for a pair of purple sunglasses. Then she wallowed around in it again for a tiny tube of something clear she smeared on those full lips. Then she practically dove in head-first to retrieve a flowered scarf thing she tied around her hair.

"What is that? A bottomless handbag?" he snapped, knowing his temper wasn't warranted, but he couldn't help himself. If she went for something else in there, he wasn't sure she'd ever come back out.

"You wouldn't believe me if I told you." She laughed, and he swore the sun shone a little brighter. "I just carry a lot of stuff. Wallet, makeup, sketchbooks, pencils, sunglasses, yarn, my loom, pocketknife, measuring tape, keys, bomb pin, glitter..."

"Glitter? Loom?" He paused a moment. "Bomb pin?"

She laughed again, a low note that hit his bones like a tuning fork. "A friend of mine joined the Air Force and when she came back from one of her early deployments, she gave me a bomb release pin. I keep it on my key chain. The glitter is because I helped teach an elementary art class last week, and I just haven't cleaned out my bag. And it's only a little hand-loom."

She pulled a smaller bag out of the big one, and showed him a loom about the size of his two fairly large hands put together, with a half-woven pattern on it.

"What's it for?"

She had begun with a blue that was nearly white, weaving ever brightening shades in gradient waves across the tightly wrapped threads. The progression of colors was simple and elegant until it reached a sudden band of dark midnight, giving the whole piece a much more somber feel to it. He wondered how it would turn out.

"I don't know yet. I'm a *norn* – a fortune teller, of sorts. We were soothsayers, back in the day, but there's not much call for soothsaying anymore. No one takes it seriously, which is kind of a relief. At least no one comes to us before great battles and asks us to sacrifice bunnies so we can read their entrails or anything. Ew." She screwed up her face before she chattered on, and something about the familiar Texas drawl – Daria told him that Carina had come up from around Odessa – of her patter was soothing. "I see things in what I weave for people sometimes. Not always. Bits of their lives make it into the weave that way, so each piece is completely unique. Anyway, I carry it around with me so I have it when inspiration hits." She grinned. "Along with everything else I haul around with me."

Rodion shook his head. Unwillingly charmed, he stared down at his left hand, which was carrying a drink holder with two cups.

"I got you a refill." He shoved the carrier at her. "It's what you always order."

Carina pulled her sunglasses down just enough that he could lose himself in that stunning green, then she fluttered her eyelashes. Honest to god fluttered them. A wash of pink flowed over her cheeks before she looked away.

"Thank you." Her voice, which had been clear and steady, dropped to an intimate whisper.

He had to move closer to hear her. Had to bend his head down to hers and breathe her in. "You're welcome."

Chapter Two

*R*odion Czernovitch was sucking up all the oxygen in town. He had to be, because the air suddenly seemed mile-high thin down here below the Mason-Dixon line.

The man was gorgeous and hot and probably really nice under that growl that kept most people at arm's length. But he was also her best friend's brother, which meant that she could only ever crush on him at a distance.

A distance that was a lot shorter right now than it had ever been before.

They lived in the same apartment building, which was really more of an old house that had been divided up into apartments. "Charming, cozy, and quaint" were the words Pandora Williams, the realtor, had used to describe the units when Carina had first moved to town. More like "crumbling, tiny, and the noisy hot water heater only works half the time."

Somehow, it had become a lot more bearable once Daria's brother moved in. They didn't talk much, and they'd never even been in each other's apartments. She'd invited him for dinner a couple of times – as a good neighbor, of course – but he'd politely turned her down. She figured he wasn't interested, and kept her crush to herself.

Now he was offering her coffee in that deep voice that made her insides wobble. She wasn't going to look a gift Russian – or free coffee – in the mouth, so she enjoyed that first sip maybe a little more than she normally would have.

Rodion drew back abruptly and frowned. After a half-block of silent walking, he spoke abruptly, as if suddenly remembering he was supposed to make polite conversation.

"You say you see things in what you weave. What did you see in this bag you made for yourself?"

Carina paused, thinking about how to explain her gift to this man who ran mostly cool with occasional flashes of Texas heat. "It's hard to see your own future. It's always changing, with every decision you make, every person you meet. When I weave for other people, it's sort of similar. I'll see possibilities, depending on the paths they take. Then I take those possibilities, and interpret them symbolically. For instance, if I see someone who has always been a homebody in some exotic locale, there will be a great change in the weave, maybe an image of the new place, or just new colors, new textures."

"Yes, but what about this one?"

The man was like a dog with a bone. He didn't give up, which she supposed was a good thing for a Border Crossing agent.

Each color, each pattern, each material, meant something to her. She'd made the base from an old pair of Wranglers that had been shredded one of the last times she did barrel racing. She'd cut her horse too far in and caught her jeans on the edge of one of the barrels, which resulted not only in ripped jeans, but with a long, uneven scar on her thigh.

She'd still finished the race in third place, bleeding like a stuck hog down into her boot.

The actual weave of the bag was made of various materials. Rags she'd torn from the remnants of old rodeo and concert t-shirts that had finally grown more holes than fabric. Pieces of quilts her family members had made, handed down and used until there was almost nothing left of them. Pockets were cut from scraps of tapestry she'd woven herself, inspired by visions that had come to her in dreams. The strap was made of the salvaged parts of a beautifully tooled bridle that had supposedly been worn by her great-great uncle's horse, Widow-Maker.

Each piece of the bag held a hint of hope, a drop of dreams. And when all the pieces came together, they told the story of her history, woven intricately with glimpses of a future even she couldn't see clearly.

She cradled the purse close to her. Her family had started out thinking of her art as a harmless indulgence, but it seemed the more successful she became, the less patient they were with her. Every time they called, they told her it was time to come back home and get her head on straight. Find a real career, work on the ranch, get married and make little *norns*. It hurt that she couldn't have a conversation longer than five minutes before someone brought up what they thought she should be doing. Pointing out her success just made them more stubborn. She thought she was past letting other people tell her how she should feel about what she made. Apparently not.

Until she felt his touch on the fingers she had wrapped tightly around the strap.

"Hey. I like the bag. It's colorful and bright. Like your hair. Like you." He moved his hand, the one he couldn't close all the way, up her arm until she felt him tug awkwardly at a curl. "Pretty."

She blinked back a sudden haze of tears at his kindness. "Thank you."

The cardboard carrier in Rodion's good left hand bobbed, and she let go of her tote to help steady it. She held the carrier with him and plucked her drink out – a Mocha de los Muertos, which was espresso, chocolate and steamed milk with faint hints of vanilla, cinnamon, orange, as well as a pinch of cayenne – then waited for him to grab his plain Decappuccino. She told herself it wasn't weird that she knew his favorite drink, too.

Rodion reclaimed the holder and tossed it into a nearby recycling bin, and they continued walking as if that inexplicable moment had never happened.

Fine. That was fine. She had to get her head straight anyway. She was happy with her life right now. She didn't need to add a surly, wounded wizard to the mix or dredge up her old insecurities.

She pasted on a smile she didn't really feel. "Daria and Katya and I are getting together tonight at Howler's. Would you like to come?"

He started to shake his head, but she hung in there. "Trick's back from his latest gig, and he's bringing his guitar. At least with both of you there, neither one will be lost in a sea of estrogen."

"I'll think about it."

They had reached the front door of the house, and Rodion pushed the door open and stood to the side to hold it for her.

"Thank you. I really hope you'll come out with us." There. She'd issued the invitation and she wouldn't push anymore.

They headed up the main stairs together, both of them careful to step to the edges of the eighth step, which sounded like a dying cat's yowl if you stepped on it in the middle. His apartment was opposite hers on the second floor, splitting the house in half. If the house had been bigger, it would have been more spacious than it sounded, but with the hall between them, they were far enough apart that noises from either one of them didn't usually disturb the other.

They parted at the top of the stairs, with him going left, and her to the right. But he paused. "I nearly forgot. Daria left something for you. She found a yarn she thought you'd like the last time she was in Nashville with Trick."

Carina would have clapped her hands if she wasn't still holding her coffee. "Terrific! I've been looking for something unique for a three-dimensional project I'm doing."

"Come on in. I'll get it for you," he said, and they stopped in front of his door while he retrieved his key. And dropped it.

Their eyes met, and she could read the frustration on his face as he clenched his jaw.

"Would you hold my coffee for me?" she asked quietly, treading carefully on the line between helping and intruding.

His square jaw flexed once before he nodded, staring straight ahead, refusing to meet her eyes. She arranged her almost empty mocha in his good hand, then bent to grab the key. She wobbled a little and put her hand on the door to steady herself as she rose, but the door didn't stay closed. It flew open under her fingers as if blown by a hurricane.

Foul, malevolent energy, so intense it took her breath away, replaced the air in her lungs with the blight of toxic gas. The force of the magic shoved her back, knocking her off her feet and into the opposite wall.

Something stalked her as she lay helpless on the floor. Something born of hellfire and the icy cruelty of death. An ill wind blew a cloak around him that hid his features – all but his eyes, which glowed a venomous green.

He reached out to her with filthy hands, encrusted with

dirt, thick black lines embedded under his broken nails like dried blood. One hand wrapped around her throat, and the other squeezed her upper arm until she thought her bones would be crushed in its grip. Symbols lit up on its skin and snaked down toward her like rivers of foul blood. The sigils poured into her arm, burning their way under her skin where she could feel them writhing in her flesh.

Carina tried to scream, but she couldn't draw in enough breath to make a sound. Every time she sucked in the poisoned air, she choked out pain. It hurt to die like this, her arm and chest and head on fire from the inside, boiling her blood, burning her alive.

Abruptly, the pressure on her body eased as if someone had shoved a boulder off of her, and fresh, clean air flowed down her throat as she coughed out the filth that had been clogging her lungs.

She could see Rodion pushing the evil thing away, holding before him a glimmering shield of light that drove the shrieking monster back step by step.

The thing stopped and stared unblinking at both of them. Its mouth opened, but its lips never moved as a voice came forth like a recording.

"Rodion Czernovitch. You took my nephew from me, the only son of my dead brother. And so I shall take from you. This woman will die if you do not return to me the shards of Gebil."

"I have nothing for you, Nazar. I do not possess what you seek."

"They are small, buried deep inside you where no one can see them, but they are there. Bring them to me, or she dies under the proklyat'ye smerti.*"*

A foul word escaped Rodion. One that she'd been thinking anyway, so they were on the same wavelength.

"Where do I find you?"

"Under the fast running blood of the earth lies the key
Behind the howling wind stands the door
In the consuming fire burns the heart of one who does not bow to Death."

"When I complete the quest, the curse will be broken?"

The creature's eyes glowed brighter. *"If you complete the quest, it will."*

"Then be ready." Rodion's sword of light, gleaming brilliant and sharp, pushed out from his hand, and the thing disintegrated into dust.

Only then did he collapse next to her.

Carina curled her body into his, there on the floor, her head tucked down by his hard abs, and coughed until she thought her throat would bleed.

He bent himself around her, surrounding her, protecting her while she pulled life back into herself with every racking breath. He folded his arms around her ribs and gently stroked, soothing away the pain with his hands and murmured Russian words. Too exhausted to cry, she simply lay there and let him hold her.

Her words burned in her throat when she finally asked, "What was that?"

"I don't know." His breath was warm on her spine, his hand hot on her side where it rested now that she was better. "Don't speak yet. Let's get you somewhere safe."

Slowly, like an old man, he came to his knees. He reached out to help her, and when she wavered, he braced her against his shoulder, a bulwark of strength rising beside her.

Twined together like kudzu, they limped across the hall to her apartment.

Chapter Three

"Key?" he asked, and it was an effort to get the word out.

"In my pocket."

Perfect. He just needed to get his hands inside the sleek, lavender jeans she wore rolled up to mid-calf. Propping her up against him with his weak arm, he delved into her front pocket and thought very fixedly about baseball.

After a moment of wishing that everything about this situation was different, he found the key, hung onto it better than he had his own, and unlocked her door, then led her inside and helped her onto the couch.

"Are you all right?" She seemed a little pale, but he didn't see blood anywhere, although her right shoulder was bright red. "Here, let me see."

She flinched, but relaxed when he gentled his touch. A band of bruises was already forming in the shape of the monster's hand.

"Can you move your arm, your elbow, your hand?"

They went through the motions of first aid until he

concluded. "I don't think the bones are broken, but I can take you to the ER if you like."

"No, I think you're right. I just hope whatever that thing poured into me doesn't make my arm turn green and fall off."

"What? It poured something into you?"

She jumped a little at his tone, and pulled on her arm. He let go reluctantly. She was so much smaller than he was. It really was amazing that the golem hadn't crushed her in its grip.

"Yeah. Light, but not... good light, you know? There were sigils on its arms and they poured into me."

Rodion cursed again.

The *proklyat'ye smerti*. A death curse. And if it had been cast with magical symbols, as Carina said, it was going to be extraordinarily difficult to remove.

Even as he thought it, a shadow moved on her arm. A dark gray tendril began to grow, swirling like the ink of a beautiful, poisonous tattoo over her pale skin.

"That can't be good."

Her light words were tight with fear. Fear he couldn't put to rest without lying to her, and he wouldn't do that.

"It's not great."

"Is it fixable?"

He hesitated and felt her muscles tense under his hand. "It is, but it's not easy."

"I didn't think it would be. What is it, anyway? What was all that about?"

Rodion blew out a deep breath. "Let me get a cloth and clean off the dirt, and I'll tell you about it."

Her kitchen was clean, but cluttered with dishes and pans in no order he could figure out. But he filled a bowl with warm water and soap, then sat down next to her with a dishcloth.

She had pushed up the torn sleeve of her shirt and was trying to see the mark.

"At least I'll finally have that tattoo I've been thinking about."

He didn't know how she did it. How she maintained anything like a sense of humor in the face of such danger. His own sense of humor, already dark, had disappeared completely after his injury.

"I don't think this is the kind of ink you really want," he answered. He didn't have anything against tattoos, but he didn't like these marks of pain on her beautiful skin. He cleaned the dirt off her arm, using the bowl to catch the small rivulets of water stained red with the local clay.

The cursed swirl remained.

She sat silent while he washed her. When he was finished, patting her arm dry as gently as he could with another cloth, she asked, "So what was that thing?"

"That was a golem."

"A what, now?" Her eyebrows were raised in question.

"It's like a giant remote control doll. You create it from clay and mud, and you can send it out to do your bidding."

"Your bidding, like killing people?"

"If that's what you ask it to do. It's actually an old Jewish legend. A rabbi could make one for the protection of a village or a town against pogroms or plagues. But even the ones that protected could go wrong and destroy what they were supposed to guard."

"Is that what happened here? A good rabbi gone wrong?"

He made a derisive sound in his throat. "I know who made this golem, and Nazar Adron is no rabbi. His ancestors used to ride out for pogroms for fun. But any kind of magic, from any source, can be corrupted."

The man who had sliced open Rodion's arm was Burian Zelitch, Nazar's slimy nephew – one of the dark fae who were manufacturing and transporting Cold Pill, a drug that only affected other supernatural creatures. The name was an anglicization of the Russian words, *koldunya pyl'*, which meant "magic dust." Rodion and his squad in the Border Crossing Patrol had finally gotten good intelligence on where the Cold Pill pipeline was coming through the border in Volshev, and they'd intercepted the gang as they tried to bring in a new shipment.

Burian – young, skinny, and vicious – had come out of the darkness beyond the Trinity River, crossing the border between the Rus fae world and the mortal world. He and his crew hadn't realized they'd been found out until they were all firmly on mortal ground. Trapped between the BCP and the river, they'd fought like cornered rats.

Rather than use a gun, Burian had pulled the great sword out of a scabbard hidden by magic, and started swinging it. BCP officers were allowed to carry a traditional shashka, a Circassian single-edged, curved saber, although Rodion was one of the few who habitually wore it. It came in handier than was expected, but few agents were trained with a sword anymore.

Burian certainly hadn't been. More than once, he'd nearly cut off his own feet with the sword that was more than half his height. But more than once, he'd also come close to cutting off Rodion's head.

Rodion was too busy defending himself at the time to realize that the sword was doing most of the work, hauling Burian's scrawny body to and fro as it defended itself. But even the best swordsman can be unlucky. And even the best sword needs an experienced arm to wield it.

The moment Rodion was able to slip inside Burian's guard, the edge of the massive blade sliced deep into Rodion's upper right arm, cutting down to the bone. The pain and shock were so great that Rodion, who had only intended to disarm the young man, ended up stabbing his own shashka straight through Burian's heart. He died instantly.

And now the his warlock uncle Nazar wanted to take revenge for Burian's death by killing an innocent.

Rodion wasn't going to let it happen. And he certainly wasn't going to let it take Carina.

"So what's our next step?"

He snorted. "There is no *our* next step. You stay here, out of harm's way, and I'll take care of this."

Absolute stillness met his pronouncement, like the moment before lightning strikes. Very carefully, he met her gaze. No longer a warm and merry green, her eyes were now the color of sea ice, and he could see icebergs dead ahead.

"I know we're not close, Rodion, but you can take your macho man, misogynistic, moronic pronouncements and shove 'em right up your —"

The knock on the door derailed her just enough that he could interrupt.

"What did I say?"

Her mouth dropped open. "Seriously? You just told me to stay put while you wander off to find some dark wizard and get zapped, while I wait at home like I'm some helpless damsel, and you can't figure out why I'm angry?"

"Oh no, I get it now." He stood to pace, and let go of the tight hold he tried to keep on the anger that sometimes felt too big to control. "You just can't wait to go out there and get killed. I can shove your corpse into that giant bag and bring it home for your family. I bet they'll love that!"

She stepped up to him and kept right on going, meeting him temper for temper, her Texas twang deepening with every word. "Oh yeah? Well, if I go with you and you die, at least I'll be smart enough to call Bubba so he can haul your carcass back to town!"

They ran out of words and glared at each other, breathing hard, and he could feel her body, only an inch away from his, practically vibrating, matching him. She was far too precious to risk, even if he knew he was being unreasonable. But right now, all he cared about was quenching the thirst that had been riding him for far too long.

They reached for each other at the same time.

Carina's flavor was more tart than sweet, spicy with anger, her lips eager and giving under his as he tunneled his fingers into her rainbow hair. She had been so close to him, and yet so far out of reach since he moved here. He'd turned down all offers to be near her because he'd been afraid he couldn't trust himself. His temper had been uneven, he constantly snarled in pain, and she'd seemed too sweet for him. Too nice to stand up to him when he got angry.

He'd been wrong about her from the beginning. She was sweet, and she was nice. But she was strong, too, and more than able to go toe to toe with him in a fight. All this time, he'd thought she was the kind of soft, biddable woman he'd have wanted before the accident. He'd been wrong. This fire-spitting artist was the sexiest thing he'd ever encountered.

She moaned and squirmed against him, her hands going to his shoulders, but she didn't shove him away. Instead, she slid her hands over to rest against his chest, pulling at his shirt, trying to get her hands under his collar where his skin burned with heat.

He pulled her closer, his hands closing over her slender back, then down to clasp her soft, denim-covered curves. He squeezed, and she tried to climb him like a tree.

Rodion spun, putting her back to the wall to help support her as he held her up with the strength of one arm. They wouldn't last long like this, and much as he regretted it, they had to get going on the solution to their problem. She keened, an eager whine, and he nearly decided that Nazar could curse himself into oblivion, just to find out what else made her make that sound. But he couldn't. The curse. Her arm.

Long unused parts of him sent a painful, throbbing ache through his body when he sucked her bottom lip in between his teeth and bit down gently. Not enough to hurt, but she stopped moving.

He opened his eyes to find her watching him. With obvious deliberation, he let her go, kissing her softly one last time before he opened his arms.

"Maybe I should let you come with me," he said. "I wouldn't have thought of having Bubba carry you home."

A familiar voice intruded from the open door. "And maybe she won't need Bubba to carry you if there's nothing left of you to bury."

Chapter Four

Carina wanted to bury her face in his shoulder and not come up until she was too old to die of embarrassment.

Daria, one of her very best friends in the whole world – and Rodion's sister – was standing in the doorway with her arms crossed.

"I'm not sure whether to be ecstatic or just puzzled," said Daria, stepping into the apartment.

"Me, neither," muttered Carina.

Rodion caught her chin between his thumb and finger. "I'm leaning toward ecstatic." His whisper was quiet, and the warm gust of his breath in her ear made her shiver.

She nodded and tried to squash down the goofy smile she knew was coming over her face.

"So what happened?" Daria, whose timing had always been impeccable before, was tromping all over her thoughts right now.

She blinked.

"What do you mean, what happened?" Rodion returned the question.

"It looks like a war zone in the hall. There are dents in the drywall and piles of dust everywhere. I thought this building was kept up better."

"It is. We just had a visit from a golem."

A new voice intruded. "A what?"

Trick, a former Army Ranger who had discovered he was a bard – a descendant of the great Welsh bard, Taliesin, who chronicled Arthur and Merlin – when he came to Nocturne Falls to visit a friend several months before, walked in behind Daria and closed the door behind him.

Perfect. Three people in her home and she hadn't been expecting company. She wasn't the tidiest of housekeepers, but she usually tried to pick up a little if there was any warning.

Her floor loom was in the midst of a project, and she'd been trying to decide on the right yarn, so there were skeins and balls of multi-hued wool scattered everywhere. And she'd fallen asleep on the couch, which meant the blankets and pillows that belonged there were flung hither and yon, as her Nana used to say. The general clutter of an artist with a magpie's eye for shiny things covered nearly every surface.

"A golem," repeated Rodion, and told Trick what he'd told her. As he spoke, he picked up little odds and ends, running his fingers over nubbly fabrics, examining chunks of glistening geodes, and sniffing bottles of fragrant oils.

"A dirt monster? I never knew there was so much I didn't know about magic."

"I don't think anyone knows it all," said Daria. "Alice Bishop, maybe. Or maybe Ms Bobbie Young back home in Volshev. They're both powerful enough to give me the shivers."

Rodion nodded. "Agreed. Both forces to be reckoned with. And their abilities – and advice – are neither cheap nor to be taken lightly."

He had buried the fingers of his stiff hand in a ball of wool and silk blend yarn that was medium blue and soft as goose down. She didn't think he noticed that he was rubbing the strands with his thumb.

"So y'all were attacked by this golem thing. Carina, are you all right?"

She shrugged, then wished she hadn't as her arm protested the movement.

"I may have been cursed. No big deal."

Daria rushed to her side. "No bid deal? Have you lost your mind?"

She pushed up her sleeve to show her friend the swirling black stain. "What did you call this thing?"

Rodion's face had returned to its usual stony expression. "The *proklyat'ye smerti*."

Daria gasped, and turned to Carina. "This is a big deal. A very big deal." Tears sprang to her eyes. "What are we going to do?"

Carina turned to Rodion with a smirk. "Yeah, Rodion. What are *we* going to do?"

He snorted. "We are going to find the cure. And find Nazar. Then I'll cut him into teeny tiny little pieces, and burn them down to ashes. And then I'll throw the ashes into the wind so he can never come together again."

Carina's eyes widened. "Not that you've thought about this at all."

"It's the best I could come up with on short notice."

"I like it," said Trick. "It's thorough."

"Y'all are terrible." Daria was examining Carina's mark. "Doesn't Katya have all those old spell books from her *Tetya* Irina?"

"Her aunt collected them." Carina remembered going to the quiet, dim old mansion to visit their friend after Aunt Irina's funeral. It seemed that every wall in the house held nothing but heavy bookcases filled with ancient, dusty tomes.

"Then she may be able to help us find a cure."

"Nazar said he'd lift the curse if I went to him with the shards of Gebil. But if you can find a cure, then I'll hunt him on my own."

"No!" The word spilled from her, along with an explosion of pain in her arm. His words hit her like the poison from the golem, choking her as she tried to work out what was wrong.

They all turned to her, shocked by her sudden outburst. Blindly, she groped for the green silk bag on the end of the coffee table. With a swipe of her good arm, she cleared a space.

"You can't leave. I know it. You can't leave me behind." She knew she sounded crazy, but her arm was on fire, the pain taking over rational thought.

Acting on instinct, she untied the knot holding the silk together, and the fabric unfolded into a square. She aligned each corner with the filigreed direction markers she had painted on the walls and, panting with pain, murmured a quick blessing, calling the elements to lend her the power she needed.

She breathed over the runestones of polished bone, giving them life, before she closed her eyes and tossed them onto the silk.

Carina opened her eyes to read the message of the runes. This curse thing wasn't kidding around.

"If you leave me, I die."

Rodion strode to where she knelt, and held out a hand to help her stand. Without a word, he wrapped his arms around her tightly. "Then I guess we didn't have to have that argument. I'm not going anywhere without you."

"Damn straight, you're not," said Trick, his own arm

around Daria. "We'll help you with whatever you need. Now, you'd better tell us the whole thing from the beginning."

They told the story together, and when they'd finished, Daria was fuming mad. At her brother.

"You idiot! What are you doing with the shards of of that evil old relic?"

"What is this Gebil thing anyway? I'm not sure I understand what y'all are talking about." It felt like Rodion and Daria were speaking in code, their shared knowledge of Russian magic leaving her on the outside.

Though maybe that's where she should be. Carina hadn't expected that kiss, hadn't expected the heat that exploded between them. And as amazing as it was, she didn't need to go tumbling head over heels for the cranky wizard while they were trying to find a way to get rid of her fun, new curse.

Rodion's blue eyes were full of shadows when he focused on Carina. "Gebil is the name of Koschei the Deathless's favorite sword. Its name means Death. It's been at his side for so long, it's developed a personality of its own. An unpleasant one. The sword isn't sentient, exactly, but it actively works to aid its master. I don't know how Burian got his hands on it, and I definitely didn't know that was the sword he was using when it cut me. And I had no idea there was any of it left inside me. It should have shown up on x-rays, unless magic swords just don't. At least it explains why this thing won't heal properly."

He shrugged his shoulder, and she felt him wince. How long had he been carrying this burden of pain?

"Where is the sword now?" asked Daria.

"I don't know. I never thought to ask about it, after. I assumed it was in the evidence lock-up, but if no one knew it was a magic sword, they wouldn't have taken precautions. It could have made its way back to its master."

They all stood silent for a moment until Trick spoke up. "Creepy sword." He shrugged. "So what's the first step?"

"We need to find Nazar. He left us clues." Rodion stood straighter, his voice growing deeper. That was what she wanted to hear. He was pulling himself together, and his confidence gave her strength. She patted him on the chest and stepped out of his embrace.

She needed to be strong for herself, so she defaulted to her usual wisecrack setting. "Why don't bad guys ever leave an address? *I'm at 717 Oak Street. Come by for coffee and death.*"

They all chuckled and some of the tension eased. "If only it were that easy, *milaya*. At least he left us clues on how to find him. The first one said, *Under the fast running blood of the earth lies the key.* Any ideas?"

"Water," said Daria immediately. "The key is under water. Under a river."

They all gaped at her.

"It's obvious. Water is the fast running blood of the earth. Duh." She crossed her eyes at her brother, and Carina smothered a laugh.

"So says the *rusalka*," returned Rodion.

"And who would know better than I?"

"She has a point, Rodion. I mean, water? Mermaid?" Carina gestured at her friend.

"Don't call her/me a mermaid," said everyone else in the room.

Carina burst out laughing. "I love getting you guys to do that!" *Rusalki* hated being referred to as mermaids – they had some longstanding issues with Hans Christian Anderson – so naturally, she liked to sneak one in every once in a while for a giggle at her friend.

And right now, she needed all the giggles she could get.

Chapter Five

Rodion and Carina walked slowly along the banks of Wolf Creek.

"How are we supposed to get to it under the water?" she asked.

He hated admitting when he didn't know the answer, so he said nothing. When they'd arrived at the creek, they'd started their search on the portion behind Daria and Trick's house. His sister always lived close to water.

Carina had opened her bag of runes when they arrived at the creek and cast them again, but nothing had changed. The signs said they had to stay together, and despite the fact that he hated bringing her into danger again, he wasn't going to gainsay the soothsayer.

Then she'd pulled out a pendulum made of simple, clear quartz wrapped in copper, and they followed where it pointed.

They'd walked for nearly an hour, going around brush when they could, hacking through it with his shashka – and he nearly wept for the blade – when they couldn't.

Walking quietly along the peaceful riverbank gave him

too much time to think about her. He couldn't get the spicy sweet taste of her out of his mind. She was supposed to be off limits, but that was before everything changed. Before the curse. Before he'd seen her courage.

Before they'd kissed. The way she'd responded to him, the way she felt in his arms... every minute, every second they were alone, all he wanted to do with kiss her and hold her again.

That death curse was putting a serious damper on his game. Passionate tongue-tangling aside, he needed to keep his hands to himself until this was over. Then maybe he'd ask her for coffee. Or sex. Or something in between.

Daria and Trick had gone to Katya's house, looking for a way to lift the curse as a back-up plan in case something happened and they couldn't find Nazar. Before they left, Trick had clapped him on the shoulder.

"You going to be all right, man?"

Rodion had nodded. "I will. But Carina... This isn't her fault. She shouldn't have gotten involved in this."

"Bad stuff happens, though. You just gotta work through it. And she's tough. She laughs, but there's a strong woman under there."

He thought about that as they walked. And he thought about the other thing Trick had given him. Before they left, the tall, lanky bard had wrapped his hands around Rodion's arm, closed his eyes and concentrated. Then he began to hum.

Power had radiated off the man and poured into Rodion's scarred wound in deep sonic vibrations. The foreign bits of metal inside him resonated to the magic of Trick's bardic voice. The ache he'd lived with for months had soothed to nothing more than a mild annoyance, easily forgotten. He'd forgotten what it was like not to be in pain.

A groan of relief had been torn from his chest as Trick let

go, and Rodion, a Rus fae to his bones, had pulled the man in for a heartfelt hug.

"Thank you."

"Anytime. I didn't know I could do that, or I'd have done it sooner. I don't know how long it'll last, though."

"Even if it's only for a minute, thank you."

Now Rodion walked by rushing water as if he was in a dream, pain free, with a beautiful, talented woman by his side.

Well, not quite by his side. He turned to find that she had stopped a few feet behind him. She leaned against a tree, her hand gripping her shoulder with a grimace that was all too familiar.

"It hurts," she whispered, her pale green eyes liquid with pain.

He wished Trick had been able to help her, too. Instead, he pulled her into his arms, the only comfort he could offer, and held her as she gave two broken sobs. After a moment, she sniffled.

"It's okay. I'm okay. I'll be all right. But I think we're close."

The pendulum swayed in her hand, spinning in a circle, but refused to point in a specific direction.

"Does that mean we're here?" he asked.

She nodded. "I think so. Let's look around."

They did, and what Rodion saw made him step back.

Wolf Creek fed into the water feature that gave the town its name, Nocturne Falls. If anyone went to the falls on a clear night with a full moon, they might be lucky enough to see a moonbow in the mist of the water.

But he'd never heard of peaceful little Wolf Creek having a maelstrom.

There wasn't enough water or tide there to create the deadly trap naturally. This one swirled in one of the wide places of the creek, its turbulent tide churning in a circle around a black hole that stank of dark magic. This hadn't been here the last time he'd walked along the creek, and because it was so far off the gentle nature hike that led to the falls, no one had seen it yet.

It made a twisted kind of sense that Nazar had buried the key at the bottom of this lethal whirlpool. If he dived in to retrieve it, he would die. And if he died, Carina wouldn't last long.

He looked down into her eyes and they spoke at the same time.

"We're screwed."

Her lips curled up at the corners, irrepressible, even in the face of death.

"Jinx. You owe me a Coke."

"If we get out of this, I'll pay up," he answered.

"You'd better. The promise of chemical sugar water might be the only thing that makes me feel better about this."

He squeezed her fingers and brought her hand up to his lips. "The only thing?"

"Maybe not the only thing." She smiled up at him, but through the flirting, he saw the shadows in her eyes.

"So, how do we get the key? Any ideas?" He'd gotten out of the habit of asking for help, but he was glad he did when she squeezed back.

They looked carefully over the bank at the roiling water, and saw a glint at the bottom of the dark center.

"I wouldn't even ask Daria to get that, and there's nothing in the water that can hurt her." *Rusalki* were tough, but black magic was bad for everyone.

Carina stepped back and reached elbow deep into her bag. There was something strange about that purse.

"I'm hungry. You hungry? Snacks help me think." She pulled out a couple of apples and offered him one, then bit into the other with a crunch. She considered the maelstrom thoughtfully as they chewed.

From upstream, the woods rustled. Something large was making its way toward them, and Rodion stepped in front of her, his shashka drawn and ready. He had practiced fighting left-handed with the sword, and though it wasn't his strongest side, he was proficient enough.

As far off the trail as they were, he wasn't expecting anyone to simply wander innocently toward a raging whirlpool.

A beast pushed through the brush, then snorted at them, his nostrils flaring wide.

The big black stallion who shook his head at them wasn't really a stallion at all. He was a kelpie. Many an unwary traveler had met his end on a kelpie's back, stuck to the horse by magic until it jumped into the water and drowned its victim. But the dark fae creature had fled the Unseelie court of Scotland, then made his way to Nocturne Falls. Trick had named him Bubba, and the kelpie had made Wolf Creek his home.

Bubba hadn't dragged anyone to their death since he'd been here, although he'd given a few people quite a scare. And he really, really liked apples.

"Bubba!" Carina took a last big bite out of her apple, then held the rest of it out to the killer fae water horse on a flat palm. He lipped at the fruit, then took it from her gently, crunching it between his big yellow teeth and drooling happily.

Rodion and Bubba had been introduced, but as someone who spent his career making sure dark fae didn't come to the mortal world, he'd never trusted the big horse.

They side-eyed each other until Rodion held out the remains of his apple, too. The kelpie didn't bite him, but it blew wetly on his hand before taking the offering.

"Gross." Rodion wiped his hand on his pants. "I don't think that thing likes me."

Carina was crooning to the horse, rubbing his poll and patting him with no fear of becoming stuck. "Nonsense. Bubba's a total sweetheart, aren't you, baby?"

"If I got stuck to him, Bubba would very happily dive right into that maelstrom and drown... me..." His voice trailed off, and he and Carina shared a look.

"He can do it," she said excitedly. "He's probably one of the few things on earth who could navigate the maelstrom and survive it."

"This might work." It might kill him, too, but he didn't share that with Carina. She wouldn't let him go if she was afraid for his life, but this was all on him. He'd drawn Nazar to them and he hadn't gotten her out of the way of the golem. This was an acceptable risk, and with Bubba's help, he had a better than even chance of surviving.

They led the kelpie to the bank.

"What do you think, Bubba?" she asked the horse. "Can you get through that?"

Bubba tilted his ears forward at the roaring whirlpool and blew out another snort, but didn't seem afraid or worried.

With a frown, he took Carina's hand in his. "We'll be separated. Will you be all right?"

"I'll be fine." She smiled at him, a hint of sparkle in her eyes. "I promise. It's only a couple of minutes, anyway. Down and back, right?"

He nodded, unsure, but she sounded so positive that he let himself be convinced. Rodion took off his sword belt, but kept the knife he had strapped to his ankle. There wasn't much else to do.

His heart was pounding, but his hands were steady. He was ready to swing onto the horse's back, but there was one thing he needed to take care of first, in case this didn't work.

With his good arm, he grabbed Carina by the waist and pulled her in, movie star style. Her eyes widened as their bodies connected, and he soaked in the sudden warmth of having her in his arms. Feeling like Errol Flynn, he braced an arm behind her shoulders and dipped her back, just enough to get her to the perfect angle. Then, with a pirate's grin, he kissed her.

Like the best of leading ladies, she responded willingly. Her arms clasped around his shoulders, and she responded to his kiss with fervor and passion. That hot sweetness – rich chocolate with a peppery bite – flowed over his tongue and through his body until he loosened his grip.

He set her back solidly on her feet, but they clung a little longer, both unwilling to let go. Finally, she stepped back.

"Come back safe," she whispered.

He nodded, and put his hand deliberately on the kelpie's withers. He tried to pull away, but he was stuck fast. There was no turning back.

Rodion mounted with a strong push, and tightened his knees around Bubba's girth. "Let's go, boy. We need that key."

With a splash, the kelpie leapt into the swirling waters of death.

Chapter Six

She was in a dream. Or maybe a movie. One where there were amazing kisses and death-defying feats of bravery. The black horse with streaming main and tail, and the dark-haired man dressed in black were beautiful together, and she worked to focus on the details because this image would appear in her dreams and in her art for the rest of her life. Rodion looked like a cavalry soldier, straight backed and elegant and determined atop a show horse, sleek and proud with an intelligent focus in his gleaming red eyes. They were ready for battle.

The kelpie jumped and they disappeared under the surface leaving no trace in the troubled waters. The mist spewed from the maelstrom was bitter and icy, covering her hair and skin with a cold dampness that seeped into her bones.

The moment they went under, flame erupted on her shoulder. The black poison swirled like the waters of the creek, covering more of her skin in its insidious pattern. She'd known this would happen, but nothing could have prepared her for the pain.

Seconds passed and she could no longer stay on her feet. Carina dropped to her knees. She pulled her arm into her body, but couldn't touch the marks with her other hand because it was like pouring gasoline on the fire in her flesh.

She wouldn't scream. She promised herself she wouldn't make a sound. In her heart, deep inside her magic, she knew that if she made so much as a squeak, Rodion would hear her and return, rather than completing his task.

So she suffered in silence, counting the seconds as they ticked on too slowly for her, but too quickly for him, stuck underwater.

A minute went by.

Thirty seconds more.

Two minutes.

This was taking too long. How long could a man hold his breath? How long until a second of life became an eternity of death?

She wasn't sure how much longer she could hold in the scream that was building inside her as she watched the marks on her arm grow thicker and longer, like a vine of the most vicious poison ivy in the world.

Carina lost track of the seconds, drowning in her own agony while tears poured down her face.

She was so out of touch with anything but the reality of her pain, she didn't see or hear Bubba and Rodion clamber back onto the bank of the creek. It wasn't until she felt his cold, wet hand cover her arm, dousing the fire, that she opened her eyes.

"You're back. You made it," she whispered.

"We did." He pulled her closer and she didn't mind the wetness that soaked her clothes, or the brush of his hand on her arm. "And with the key."

He held up the ornate key to show her. It was beautiful. Shining gold with two simple teeth at the bottom, the top was a fantastically delicate knotwork of metal with a thumb-sized cabochon ruby embedded in its center. It was too lovely to be mixed up in this mess of hurt, but she figured that was how things were sometimes. Pretty things covered up the ugly.

Philosophy and pain. She was going to need a towel. And an ibuprofen. And more coffee.

Rodion's chest heaved with each breath, and she put her hand – the one she could move without flaming swords of agony shooting through it – against him to help calm him. She wouldn't lie. It soothed her to touch him, too.

"Are you all right?" she asked. "How's Bubba?"

"We're fine, but I wouldn't have made it without him. I thought the tide would rip me right off his back, but when you're stuck to a kelpie, you're stuck." His words were filled with grudging admiration, and Bubba gave him a shove with his nose. "Yeah, yeah. Thank you. I appreciate the help."

Carina winced and Bubba waited. Thanking a fae, especially an Unseelie fae, came at a cost.

"How about apples for the next two months? Or maybe seaweed. Some of that crunchy dried sushi paper? Trick said you like that."

Bubba gave a shaking nod of his huge head, splattering water everywhere like a massive wet dog, and the deal was struck.

Rodion put his hand on the kelpie's forehead to scratch for a moment before Bubba stepped away and trotted back to the creek. Without pausing, he jumped in, downstream of the whirlpool that was slowing back to its usual slow roll, and disappeared under the water.

Carina was shivering and Rodion wrapped her in his arms and led her to sit with him, leaning against the bole of a cottonwood tree to watch the water return to its peaceful flow and let the pain in her arm ebb away.

"I don't know what you packed in here," he said, pulling her bag close. "Do you have anything to warm you up?"

Using her good hand, she rummaged around until she touched the edge of a cotton blanket she'd woven years ago when she was just learning. The threads were loose in some places and too tight in others – she'd just been learning how to use the warp and weft – and her vision of the pattern hadn't exactly come out like she'd planned. It was supposed to have stars on it, but they were more like blobs of uneven color. No matter. It was her first, and as ugly as it was, it was also really soft after so many washings.

She pulled it out, and felt the quiet rumble and puff of air that passed for his laughter. "There's something really weird about that blanket. And that bag."

She smiled to herself. It was her favorite secret. Every piece of yarn and fabric she'd woven into the cloth had been soaked for a month – full moon to full moon – in a stretching spell. Essentially, each piece could cover a mile for each inch of length. The work had exhausted her, but it was more than worth the effort it had taken to make the bag. It could hold literally anything she'd ever need, and still look super cute at the same time.

Before they came out today, she had packed a few essentials while Rodion went to cover himself in weapons. She'd put in an extra pair of comfy sneakers and dry socks, her favorite blanket, and a handful of the protection charms she had strewn about her apartment. Then came her favorite bag of runestones, and a small box containing the fragile set of casting bones passed down from a several generations of great-grandmothers. Like Hermione Granger, she stashed a few pertinent spell books in there. Unlike Hermione, she did not pack a tent. She didn't care how nice it was, or that she'd been raised on a ranch and slept under the wide Western sky too many nights to count. Carina Valdis was not the kind of woman who slept in tents if there was a hotel within fifty miles.

But right now, she needed warmth. With a fierce Russian warrior at her back, she draped the soft cotton blanket over both of them and they dozed in the shade in the heat of the day.

Carina woke disoriented and stiff, laying alone in the grass with the blanket twisted around her waist. When her eyes cleared, she realized she was looking at Rodion's back.

His naked back.

He had taken off his shirt and she saw it hung over a branch, air drying, while he was hunched over something in his lap. A rhythmic metallic scrape sang through the air.

Carina had taken a few life drawing classes in college, but not one of the models had been built like Rodion Czernovitch. Each muscle was cleanly sculpted, its purpose clear as he shifted and moved, his good arm sweeping out steadily.

A symphony of movement under his skin. A god made flesh. Yet despite his beauty, he wasn't perfect. Scars marred his back, and from where she sat, she could finally see the one that had brought him to Nocturne Falls.

She'd heard that it was a knife wound, so she'd expected a neat, narrow slash. She was completely unprepared for the wide, gaping silver mark that covered the top of his arm. Nor was she ready for the scar to be so bubbled and uneven, a sign of poor healing.

He must have heard her slight gasp, because he turned and caught her staring at his arm. Defensively, he covered it with his hand.

Carina reached out. "Please don't. I'm sorry. It was rude of me to stare, but I hadn't seen it before."

He stared down at her, his eyes icy cold. "Ugly, isn't it?"

"Are there pretty scars?"

This time his huff of breath wasn't quite what she would call a laugh. It was too bitter for that. Time to get his mind off his wound.

"What are you working on?" She got on all fours and crawled the few feet toward him. His eyes flashed from ice to hot blue flame in a blink.

She smiled.

Carina wasn't dumb. She knew how her prowl affected him, and she laughed, quiet and low and inviting, at his reaction.

When she reached his side, he put aside the blade he was sharpening and pulled her into his lap. "I think I'll work on you."

They surfaced for air some time later, her lips swollen and tender, feeling very pleasurably mussed. She reached up to wipe away a smudge of shimmery berry lip gloss, and gave him a satisfied grin.

"That was fun."

"It was," he agreed. "We should do it again."

Something about he way he said it made her tilt her head. He was looking at every part of her face. Staring, actually, like he was trying to memorize her. And she realized there was a difference in his expression. The little line that habitually bisected his eyebrows wasn't there anymore, or at least it was relaxed. There was no tension in his face. She pressed her thumbs lightly at the base of his neck, and though the muscles were hard, they weren't locked tight.

So this was what Rodion looked like when he was relaxed and open. She'd never seen him like this before. And she'd been the one who helped make him this way

She sat quietly in his lap, too, with no desire to move. That was something else rare. She'd never been the type to linger over caresses. She was usually too restless, but right now, she didn't want to move away from his steady gaze, and his hand rubbing circles on her back.

"I don't want to move," he murmured. "But we have to. We're not done, and I'm not going to let Nazar, or anyone, take you away from me."

She wanted to say "Same," but emotion welled up and choked her, so she just nodded into his chest.

They gathered up their things and she folded her blanket, stuffing it down into her bag.

"So. Howling winds." She peered at him through narrowed eyes. "Where in the world are we going to find howling winds?"

Chapter Seven

It was a good question. One they pondered and discussed as they walked back to Daria and Trick's home. The two were standing on the back porch, arms wrapped around each other, as he and Carina walked up from the creek.

He was glad for Daria. She'd gone through enough with her stalker from years ago, and Trick had been instrumental in making sure his sister was safe. It was only a matter of time before wedding bells rang for the couple, he was sure.

"You look like you went for a swim," Trick called as they approached.

"It wasn't fun, but it was necessary. And now I owe Bubba apples and nori for two months."

"Don't try to cheap out with Red Delicious. He'll step on you. He likes Honeycrisps, but Braeburns will do in a pinch. And don't get the nori chips with sesame oil in them. I bought those once by accident. He ripped the sleeve clean off my jacket. Never touched me, but I miss that coat."

Rodion's brow went up. Bubba was pretty picky for a horse. "Good to know. Did you find anything at Katya's?"

Daria shook her head. "Nothing. She's still looking, but we were hoping we might catch y'all here." The breeze was picking up – unseasonably cool for May – and Carina shivered. Rodion stepped to her other side to block the blowing air.

"Come on in," said Daria. "I'll make some…" Her voice trailed off as she looked up.

A massive black crow tumbled across the sky, cawing and flapping, trying to right itself as it was pushed in front of a gale force wind.

The bird saw them and angled downward, falling out of the sky until it landed at their feet. Immediately, the crow transformed into a familiar man.

That is to say, a man they knew who was also a witch's familiar – Pandora's fiancé, Cole, an advanced math teacher at Harmswood Academy.

"Not cool, you guys!" Cole straightened his glasses, ran fingers through his messy hair, and pulled his shirt down. "Whichever one of you did that, it's not funny!"

Since they were all staring at the man with uniform expressions of dismay, Rodion spoke up. "The wind? That wasn't us, Cole. What happened to you?"

"Magic happened," he griped, not that anyone blamed him. "And not the kind of magic from Pandora or her family."

Another gust knocked everyone back a step. The sky had turned ominously dark, the eerie gray-green that often heralded tornadoes or hailstorms. But this didn't feel like a regular storm. Tainted magic weighed heavy in the air, fouling the atmosphere with ozone.

The howling winds were here.

As one, they all turned and ran for the house. Trick struggled to shut the door, and Cole and Rodion threw their weight behind it until the latch clicked firmly.

Carina dug in her bag and soon came up with a handful of small, shining bits of stone and wire. She immediately began to hang them on the hinges, the lock and the knob, murmuring over each one as she placed them. "Wards for protection. Here. Place one at every window and door. Anywhere the wind can blow through."

Everyone took a few and they scattered through the house, placing the tiny talismans at every opening. Trick followed, singing a few words over each one to strengthen the wards. When they gathered back in the living room, they took a moment to breathe.

"What. The hell. Was that?" Cole glared at all of them.

Rodion felt for the man. He'd literally been blown into their midst and had no idea what was going on.

Daria piped up. "I'll make tea. I feel like tea will help. Rodion, why don't you fill in the details?"

Trick shrugged and went to the kitchen with her.

Rodion and Carina sat in the living room with the professor and brought him up to where they'd left the others this morning. Daria came back with a steaming pot of tea, mugs, honey and milk. As she poured, they caught up with the part about the maelstrom in the creek.

"And I thought being blown around by a rogue breeze was bad," said Cole as he sat back with his cup.

The wind beat against the doors and windows in fits and starts, and Rodion watched Carina look outside nervously. He put his hand on her knee and she jumped a little at the touch.

"It will be all right, *milaya*. Soon, this will be only a memory."

She smiled a little at his words, but he meant every one of them. He'd do anything to keep her safe. She had no idea how far he'd go for her.

This morning, she'd been a neighbor he'd wanted to get

to know better. Well, he got his wish. And what he'd discovered today during some of the most difficult times he'd seen anyone take on, was that she wasn't just pretty and smart and creative and artistic. She also had backbone like he'd rarely seen, even amongst his own team.

She put a hand over her arm and grimaced. "I could do without the killer tattoo, that's for sure."

He barely held back a snort. And she was funny. He liked that dry and slightly dark sense of humor. It was very Russian.

"What happened, Cole?" asked Daria, doctoring her own cup of tea. "How did you get caught in that?"

"It's a long weekend at the academy, so I thought I'd take some time off and do a little flying. Check out some of Pandora's properties, just look over town. Gargoyles and dragons get noticed. Crows, not so much." He shrugged. "I was over by the town square and spotted something kicking up dust. And, well, I saw something shiny."

Carina smiled into the steam from her tea. "You are a crow, after all."

He grinned, and Rodion tightened his fingers on her knee. Carina glanced at him with an eyebrow raised and he forced himself to loosen his grip. The instinctive jealousy was neither necessary nor productive. He knew better.

"Anyway, I got sucked right into the thing. It wasn't really a tornado, and it wasn't touching down or doing any damage, it just carried me away. It seemed to be sweeping over the town, like it was looking for something. I'd just gotten a little ahead of it when I saw you guys, and figured I'd better get out if I could. So here I am. Now, does anyone know what that thing is and what it's after?"

"*Vikhor*." Rodion grated out. "I know exactly what it is. Nazar has harnessed the spirit of the whirlwind."

"And he's sent it out, like another golem?" asked Carina.

"No, he has to let the *vikhor* into him to use its energy. He's actually inside it. Which means he has come to us." Satisfaction bled into his words. "We may be able to end this sooner than we thought."

"Wait, what do you mean?" She put down her tea and the liquid sloshed up to the rim. "We're only supposed to find a door behind it, but you're going to go fight the wind? This is a terrible idea."

"Nazar still needs me if he wants those shards. They must be taken from me alive, otherwise, he'd have already hired a sniper and done the deed as soon as he knew where I was."

She paled, then crossed her arms and glared at him. "This is not filling me with confidence, Rodion."

"I'll be fine." He'd make sure of it, to protect her.

"I don't like it. I don't like that he found us, and I really don't like that he's some sort of mad wizard tornado spirit."

There wasn't anything he could say to ease her mind. And in truth, he wasn't sure that Nazar wouldn't kill him. It's possible the old wizard simply wanted the chance to bathe in his blood himself, rather than hire it done from afar.

Part of him bristled that she didn't trust him to take care of himself, the bigger part of him got that her fear for him didn't stem from her thinking he was weak, but that she didn't want the worst to happen. He'd moved away from Volshev to get away from women who wanted to smother him in their protection and their fear.

But much like Daria, Carina wasn't going to try to stop him. She wasn't going to stand in his way while he did what he needed to do.

He opened his arms and she leaned into them, wrapping herself around him. The smell of her shampoo drifted up, and he hoped he would bear the imprint of her body as he walked out to meet battle, that he could carry her scent and her warmth with him like a *bogatyr* of old carried his lady's favor.

He tilted her chin up until he could look straight into her jade-green eyes, then bent to take her mouth.

Like before, the bite mixed with the sweet. He traced a hand down her back, loving the curves that were soft under his touch, the strength under the silk of her skin, the electric heat that melted from her body into his.

He didn't notice until her face was buried in his neck that they were now alone in the living room. Voices drifted to him from the kitchen, and he was grateful for their tact in leaving him alone with Carina for this moment.

"Cast your runes, *milaya*," he whispered in her ear. "Tell me my fortune. But no matter what the bones say, know that I will come back to you."

"Come back to me?" She pulled out of his arms, and he could see he'd said something to upset her. Again. "You think I'm going to let you go out there alone? Didn't we already have this conversation?"

He nodded cautiously. "Yes. And I can do this on my own. I don't need your protection. And you can't fight it. You don't have the weapons and you're wounded."

Her jaw dropped, and he took a wary half-step back.

"I'm wounded," she said, and he thought he might have made a mistake bringing it up. "*I'm* wounded," she repeated with emphasis.

He'd definitely made a mistake.

"You arrogant, delusional, one-armed, half-wit." He didn't realize he'd been backing up until she started stalking him. "What makes you think you need to go out there alone? Why wouldn't you have help? What are you gonna do, anyway? Shoot it? Stab it?"

"Actually, yes."

She stopped. "I beg your pardon?"

"That's how you stop the *vikhor*. If you can stab it or slash it through the heart, the sorcerer inside it will be wounded. If I can wound Nazar, I can capture him. And if I can capture him, I can get him to release you from the curse."

Carina squinted at him thoughtfully. "You're still arrogant. And one-armed. And probably delusional."

"Yes. But not a half-wit?" He tried a tentative smile.

She frowned at him. "Well, you don't seem to learn very quickly. I'd better come with you, just in case."

Every protective instinct in him surged forward. What was it with this woman needing to charge into danger? "The hell you are."

"The hell I'm not," she snapped back. "We can't be separated. Remember what happened at the creek? Anyway, I can distract him."

"You mean tempt him to kill you?" He refused to let her put herself in harm's way. Stubborn woman. Couldn't she see he needed to keep her safe after he'd been the cause of so much damage already?

Without any regard at all for her life or his sanity, she continued blithely. "He's not going to kill me. Like you said, Nazar needs me alive. At least for now. I'm the bait on the hook he set for you. If I die too soon, he knows you won't give him what he wants."

"You're not going out there. What are you going to do? Throw glitter and wool at him?" He made his words deliberately insulting, but she simply lifted a perfect eyebrow.

"Actually, yes."

She was repeating his earlier words, and he found he didn't like it at all. "I beg your pardon?"

"You know I used to compete in junior rodeo, right? Calf roping. If there's really a person in the middle of that whirlwind, someone you can stab, then it's someone I can rope."

"This isn't some Texas tall tale. You're not Pecos Bill."

"You mean Great-Great Uncle Bill?"

They could have heard a pin drop all the way through the house. The sounds from the kitchen had stopped, and even the walls seemed to be holding their breath. She couldn't be serious. "Great-Great Uncle Bill?"

"You didn't think those stories were all just made up, did you?" She smirked at him and irritation crawled all over his skin. "Sugar, don't forget I'm from Odessa. The one in West Texas, not the one in Ukraine."

Rodion stalked over to her. "I thought you were a *norn*. A Nordic soothsayer."

"I am. From my mom's side of the family. But the Vardis's have been all over Texas for a much longer time than anyone can imagine."

"And you want to rope the whirlwind?"

"You want to stab it. Seems fair to me."

He reached for her again. "We're both insane."

She nodded into his chest. "But our crazies fit together pretty well."

Chapter Eight

Carina was sure they were both going to die. But at least this way, she'd be going out doing something, not just waiting around for some sneaky spell to cut her off before she was ready.

Out of her bag, she pulled a skein of wool/silk blended yarn, the color a perfect match to Rodion's piercing blue eyes. It was the one he'd buried his hand in back at her apartment.

Cutting the skein into nine pieces of equal length, she set Daria to braiding one set, Trick and Cole to another, and she had Rodion hold one end of her braid. Once those were done, she braided all three braids together one more time to create a thick, flexible rope about ten yards long.

Too flexible.

"This thing's as limp as something I shouldn't say in mixed company."

Cole snorted tea out of his nose, and Daria whacked Trick on the back as he gasped for breath. But Rodion leaned over and whispered, "Not on me, *milaya*."

She choked a little on that, but recovered. She wouldn't look, she wouldn't look...

She looked.

The man was not wrong.

After their necking session on the creek bank, she had a good feeling about where their ... relationship? She wasn't sure what to call it. But she liked where it was going. Not to bed yet, of course. They had to live through this curse thing first. But since she was pretty sure he hadn't stuffed any socks down his pants... Well, it was something to look forward to.

Ahem. Anyway.

She taped off the ends of the thick braid. "I wove some warding spells and some small talismans into the wool, but I need this to be sturdier. Not completely stiff because I still have to loop and swing it, but this is too stretchy." She looked around at the assorted magical and mystical people. "So, who can help?"

Trick shook his head. "Sorry. I sing. I have some influence over how people feel, but I don't really have physical powers."

"Water magic, sweetie. I'm no help here." Daria wiggled her fingers with a regretful frown.

"I'm a familiar." Cole shrugged helplessly. "I amplify Pandora's spells, but I don't have any powers of my own, other than the shift."

That left Rodion. The fingers on his weak hand clenched over and over, curving slightly and flexing, but not making a full fist.

"I don't know. Ever since this happened, I've had trouble controlling my magic. The shield I used earlier is something I haven't been able to call since I was wounded. A few months ago, I could have done what you asked. Now?" His voice trailed off, and he frowned fiercely at the floor.

Cole stepped up and put a hand on Rodion's shoulder. "I might be able to help. I'm obviously bonded to Pandora, but there may be a way for me to help boost your abilities."

"It could work." Rodion nodded. "Trick, I may need your help, too."

"Whatever you need, brother."

Carina and Daria stood back as the three men stood together in the living room, shoulder to shoulder. Her eyes clouded up, and as she looked over at one of her best friends in the world, she saw that Daria was a little weepy, too.

"They look good together, don't they?"

Carina nodded. She hadn't been sure that Rodion would accept help from anyone, but she felt sure that, together, the men could find a way to make this work.

Rodion held the woolen braid in his hands. Trick had both of his hands wrapped around Rodion's injured arm, and hummed, low and steady. And Cole had one hand on Rodion's other shoulder, lending support.

In the midst, Carina watched and listened as Rodion chanted in Russian. Daria translated the call for strength and suppleness to harness the wind, and to protect and defend the one who held the rope.

Under his increasingly agile fingers, the rope slowly transformed. What had once been lovely but without form became a glittering tool with the strength needed to take on evil.

At the end, the men were all sweating. Trick hadn't stopped his song the entire time, and Rodion's hand moved better than she'd ever seen it.

"I didn't know Trick could do that," whispered Daria in tears. "My poor brother suffered all this time, and we didn't know."

Carina pulled her friend in for a hug. "But we know it now. And now is when he really needed it."

Cole was panting lightly, too. The bespectacled math professor swiped a hand over his brow. "I've never done that with anyone but Pandora. I hope it helped."

"It did. Both of you." Rodion held out the shining blue lariat to Carina. "I haven't been able to focus my magic since the injury. This was amazing. Thank you, my friends."

The men pulled each other in for brief, back-pounding bro-hugs, then separated.

Trick squinted at the cloud outside. "But I have to say, the best thanks would be getting rid of that dust devil in my back yard. If it rips up the roses Daria just planted, I'm not responsible for what happens."

Rodion held out the rope to Carina. "Ready?"

"I am. Do you need to rest or something?"

"I feel better than I have in months." His smile came easier and it made her heart skip a beat.

"Then I guess I'm ready when you are."

She was letting Rodion's enthusiasm and renewed strength carry her, because she was honestly terrified. It had been a while since she swung a rope. Junior rodeo champion had been a long time ago. But she had to have faith. She swung and twirled the rope around her, getting used to its weight and balance, wishing she had a horse under her.

He watched, and she could feel his scrutiny. After a few minutes, however, the rhythm of the rope pulled her in, and she flowed with the movement. Soon, she tried her old rope tricks, a flat loop, spinning the rope around her body in a merry-go-round, standing inside the spinning loop, then spoke jumping where she stepped in and out of the rope. She switched to vertical loop, and once she got the loop wide enough, she was able to jump through it from side to side, a move called the Texas Skip. Finally, she started a butterfly swing that she bounced up her arm, then to her shoulder, and finally over her neck.

Her friends laughed and clapped, and the familiarity of the rope put her at ease. She could do this.

But before she rolled up her rope and put it away, she widened the loop and sent it flying over Rodion. It closed loosely around his shoulders and she tugged at it, bringing him close.

"Nice trick, *milaya*. You have a lot of hidden skills. Maybe someday you can tie me down where we don't have an audience." He winked, and she felt the blush burn through her.

"I do not need to hear that about my brother and my friend. Ew," Daria teased.

Rodion's laugh was a low rumble that made his bright eyes squint and his white teeth flash. It warmed her from the inside out, listening to his joy.

"Now I feel like I should show you what I can do." He nodded at his sister. "Would you sing?"

Carina had heard Daria sing before. The first time was with Trick, on the little stage at Howler's. Since then, she'd heard bits and pieces of music, often recordings Daria had made years ago with her family's Russian folk/pop music group, Sirenas. But she'd never heard her friend like this.

It was easy to forget that Daria was Russian sometimes. She had almost no accent left, and even though she'd heard Daria and Katya speak to each other in Russian before, Daria seemed a little disconnected from her heritage. It could have been a result of the way she cut herself off from her family to run from her stalker.

This was the first time Carina heard her friend sing as a *rusalka*. The Russian siren began low, her voice at the very bottom of her register. Daria's eyes closed and her shoulders began to move in rhythm with the song. She snapped her fingers, and Trick caught the beat, slapping his hands on his thighs as she sang a martial tune that Carina had imagined could inspire wave upon wave of soldiers to march straight into battle. As she sang, her fiancé began to hum, giving the song a bass thrum.

And before her eyes, Rodion became more than the neighbor, more than the soldier, more than the man with the smoking hot kisses.

He became martial beauty. The shashka rang as it came free of its scabbard and began to twirl back and forth, round and round, until it was a gleaming blur. The insistent beat of the song rose higher and higher, and Rodion began to move, weaving in time with the music, pushing himself into the rhythm.

He spun the blade with his left hand, attacking phantom opponents on all sides, stabbing and slashing high and low before he passed the saber to his right hand. For a moment, the movement faltered. Daria's song slowed, and as before, he began to twirl the blade, repeating the motions he'd already done, but with the arm that had been wounded.

It took longer for him to get up to speed, but when he did, he surpassed the dangerous dance he'd done the first time, using both arms to create new patterns and slay new enemies. And all the while, Daria's haunting wail recalled an ancient ethos of savage bravery.

The song ended, and Rodion stood, chest heaving. He clapped a hand over his bad shoulder and Carina went to him with a bottle of cold water that Cole had brought out.

He guzzled it down, and his breathing returned to normal. "So, we're a good team, yes?"

His accent was back, thicker than usual, and it sent a thrill through her, warming up the parts of her body that responded to strong, capable warriors. It seemed he was finally learning that she didn't need a man to stand in front of her, but beside her. That was incredibly sexy.

"Like I said," she answered. "Our crazies match."

Chapter Nine

They stood outside the door, side by side. Rodion, armed with the shashka handed down from his grandfather, the blade gleaming with its own light. Carina, with loops of glittering rope in her hand. She had braided her hair as efficiently as she'd braided the rope, and the streaks of blue, purple and pink shot color through the bright blonde.

They were the only spots of light in the grim mid-day darkness that awaited them. Trees swayed violently, and above the rush of gusting wind, he could hear branches cracking and breaking.

"It's a little breezy out!" She had to yell the words at him, just to be heard over the storm. Her short sleeves flapping like tiny wings, exposing the black swirls on her arm.

He shrugged and shouted back at her. "I may be Russian, but I've spent a long time in Texas. This is nothing more than a little spring breeze!"

Apparently, the *vikhor* was offended by that, and the wind pushed him back a half step. Carina put a hand up to her eyes, but bent at the knees and leaned into it. She smiled grimly at him.

Together, they walked into the open. She got up on her toes and spoke into his ear. "What exactly am I looking for?"

"A sort of solid-feeling center. Most of this is just noise and flailing around, but it's coming from somewhere. You'll feel it when you get there."

She nodded and he reached down to squeeze her hand, thanking all the gods for the gift of being able to use his fingers again, especially to touch this woman.

But it was time to work now, so he let go of her hand, and they stepped away from each other. Out of the corner of his eye, he watched her shake out a loop and begin a rhythmic swing.

He did the same thing with his sword. Daria's song – an old soldier's ballad of bravery and savage ferocity – played in his head as he began an easy twirl, hand over hand, side to side. The unsharpened portion of the blade near the hilt, called the ricasso, rolled over his hand smoothly as he became one with the deadly movement. The rest of the saber was razor sharp, and the blade bayed like a hunting dog as he picked up speed. The repetitive sway cleared his mind of everything but his prey.

Around and around they walked, into the wind, buffeted by its force. The wind reached out and whipped at them, flaying their exposed skin with dust and sand, sucking the breath away from them to make them gasp, then pushing too much at them until breathing was like drinking from a fire hose.

Nazar wanted him dead, but Rodion wasn't going to let the old sorcerer take Carina with him. They had to find the door.

He pushed into a strong gust and suddenly felt the wind

falter – just the slightest bit – when he walked into something solid. He'd found it. The heart of the whirlwind.

As soon as he touched it, the shards in his arm began to burn like fire. His fingers stiffened in pain and he nearly dropped his sword. He didn't mean to shout out loud, but Carina heard him.

"Rodion! Are you all right?"

He looked over and fury rolled through him. Blood smeared her lip and chin and the back of her hand where she'd tried to wipe it away.

"What happened to you?"

"It's nothing," she yelled out, trying to be heard over the wind. "A pebble hit me. Are you all right?"

He nodded back, lying to her. His right arm was useless again, the pain numbing his arm and hand as if they'd been dipped in lava, leaving behind nothing but cold fire.

He sneered at the wind, tightened his left-handed grip on the blade and stood firm.

"Is that the best you can do?" he yelled into the *vikhor*. It pushed harder and he shoved back, determined to stay on his feet. Carina leaned forward, trying to keep her balance.

"Is this it?" she asked, her voice loud and hoarse.

He nodded. "Come up on my right and let's give it a whirl."

She grinned at his pun and swiped at the blood on her face again. "Anyone ever tell you that your sense of humor is a little loopy?"

Roping puns. He'd happily listen to her terrible jokes for the rest of his life. If they lived through this. Which reminded him…

"When this is over, I'm going to kiss you again."

"Then I guess we'd better get the job done," she called back. She winked one green eye, then shook out another loop on her rope, enlarging the center. The magic worked into the rope kept it steady, even in the face of the raging wind, so he left her to her business while he faced the center of the storm.

"You hide in the *vikhor*, Nazar. Come out and face me. At least Burian had enough courage for that."

"And it got the stupid boy killed!" the wind roared back.

He kept talking, taunting the storm, and keeping his senses trained on the center of energy that he'd found. All the while he watched Carina fight the gale as she moved around the *vikhor*, her rope twirling at her side.

Quick as a striking snake, the loop widened and swung out into the whirling center of the storm. There was every chance she was going to miss. She was trying to rope the wind, after all, and no matter who her great-great uncle had been, it was still the stuff of tall tales. Nonetheless, he held his breath for a moment, watching the gleaming blue of the rope fly out... and catch.

Nazar roared in fury as his body became visible, a line of blue pulled tight over his neck and one shoulder. In his free hand, Rodion could see a bright ball of flame pulling together to fling at the woman who had caught him.

His own battle cry ripping from his throat, Rodion charged the sorcerer, using all his skill and strength to strike down his enemy. With a whirling leap, he sliced deep into the tempest around Nazar, then spun back to face him again.

Wounded and trapped, the wizard lost control of the *vikhor*. The whirlwind spirit pulled away from the sorcerer and spun off into the clouds, leaving behind a rippling whirl of dust and leaves and a hint of magic.

And there in the dirt lay a dark-haired man with silver streaks at his temples and cruelty like black fire in his eyes. Blood pooled beneath him, but he wasn't dead.

Carina's rope was pulled tight around his body and he struggled against the binding as she used the other end of the rope to tie him. In seconds, the wizard Nazar was bound hand and foot like a bawling calf.

Then she shoved back from the rope and stumbled, crying out.

Her arm was encased in thick black lines that he could see moving on her skin, staining her, causing her the same agony he'd felt as the shards of Gebil burned inside him.

Nazar, the sadistic bastard, laughed. A weak wheeze that still managed to breathe evil into the world.

Rodion caught her before she fell, then lowered her to the ground. He pulled her into his lap and looked down at her pale face.

"Carina, are you all right?"

Her beautiful eyes opened, lines of pain creasing the corners. "You know, I don't think so. Not right now."

He wrapped his arms around her, carefully avoiding touching the black poison, and hugged her close. "You have to stay with me."

Tears leaked from her eyes, and when she caught her breath in a sob, he wanted to weep with her. "I'll try, but Rodion, it burns. All the way inside."

She was hot under his hands, a dry, sickly, feverish heat that he could feel radiating out from her arm. But at her words, his heart stuttered. Carefully, he pulled aside the collar of her shirt.

The black had spread. Not just down her arm, but past her shoulder, up her neck and over her chest.

He muttered a foul word, and miraculously, Carina chuckled. "That's just what I was thinking."

"Shh," he soothed her, smoothing back her hair. Tiny tendrils had come loose from her braid, and he tucked them behind her ear. "You'll be all right." But he couldn't hide the dismay on his face from her.

"You're a terrible liar."

"I'm not lying, *milaya*. I'll do anything to make this right."

She nodded, tears making tracks in the dirt and blood on her cheeks. He laid her down in the grass, making her as comfortable as he could, before he stalked back over to Nazar.

The sorcerer had been watching them, and now he coughed out a broken laugh, a demented, wounded old man. "You may have caught me, but you haven't fulfilled the terms of the curse. I told you what you had to do."

"Let her go, Nazar."

"Like you let Burian go?"

Rodion knew he wouldn't win this argument. There was no reasoning with madmen, but he tried anyway. "He was trying to kill me. I wouldn't let him spread his poison in Volshev, and he thought it was worth fighting me."

"It wasn't worth his life!"

Rodion shook his head. Nazar was right about that. He'd known from the moment Burian had charged him that it would end badly. The young man hadn't been skilled, but looking back, Rodion realized he had been scared. As if what awaited him if he failed was worth than death. "No, it wasn't. But he didn't give me much choice. Now heal her!"

"No." The sorcerer curled his lip. "I wouldn't even if I could. You have one more quest to finish. And she might not make it. Then you'll know how I suffer."

Cold hatred filled him. "If she dies, I'll make sure you suffer like no man has ever known."

Chapter Ten

This was a Rodion she'd never seen before, and she didn't like it. Gruff, rude and curt, she could handle. But this promise of vengeance frightened her.

Inside her, she could feel the poison spreading, hot fingers stabbing deep, tainting her organs. She couldn't die now. She had too much to do. She had to make sure that Rodion didn't become the monster she was seeing now.

Carina reached for him, and he was by her side immediately.

"What do you need, *milaya*?"

"I need for you not to kill him. No matter what happens."

"I can't promise that."

"Too bad. You have to, or I swear I'll haunt you. And not in a romantic Demi Moore and Patrick Swayze kind of way. It'll be like that Ring chick with the creepy walk."

The laugh that burst out of him wasn't pretty, but it did the job. The darkness in his eyes faded away and he held her close. His warmth seeped through her skin and the black tendrils inside her retreated a little. She reached up to cup his rough cheek in her hand.

"Don't leave me," he whispered.

"I'll try."

For a moment, all was still and perfect.

Then Nazar gave a hacking cough and ruined it. Mood killer.

Rodion's warmth – and maybe a little of his magic – was making her feel strong enough to sit up on her own, but she didn't want to move away from him. Instead, she wiggled around until he was sitting cross legged, and she sat facing him, her legs wrapped around his really nicely superbly muscled tush.

His hands found a resting place on her hips, and by the time she was settled, there was heat in his eyes, as well as his hands.

She grinned.

"Feeling better?" he asked, those hard lips tilting up on one side.

"Much better. Every time we touch, it makes me stronger."

His little smile turned into a leer.

"Then how much touching would it take to heal you?" As he spoke, his fingers made their way under her t-shirt. The feel of his rough skin against her back made her gasp and arch toward him.

"If that's how this works, I'm all for it."

He pulled her forward to nuzzle his lips against her throat, and she couldn't quite hold back her moan. When he licked his way up to her jaw, she gasped and moved closer.

And when Nazar coughed again, they both groaned. He dropped his head to her shoulder.

"Timing. We need to work on our timing."

The silkiness of his hair tickled her neck, and she rubbed her cheek against him. "Stupid evil wizards."

"Yeah. Stupid evil wizards," he repeated, planting one

more soft kiss on her neck. Then he pushed back a little, taking his hands out from under her shirt. It left a cold spot on her skin. "Feeling better?"

Carina sighed and nodded. "I am. Not great, but better." She pulled aside the collar of her t-shirt to examine her super-creepy tattoo. "I think it retreated a little. It still burns, but not as badly."

He examined it with her. Or at least he looked down her shirt. His fingers tightened on her hips.

"Rodion?"

"Yup. Looks better." His voice was a little strangled, and she held in a chuckle. There was a decent amount of real estate to look at down there. Not excessive, but neither she nor any previous admirers had ever been disappointed. At least she was wearing one of her good bras today. A supportive foundation garment made everything better. And a little satin and lace didn't hurt.

She let him off the hook and crawled slowly off his lap. Not to tease him, but just because she was still weak and tired. He helped her stand with one hand under her elbow until she was steady on her feet.

Carina walked over to Nazar, then slowly knelt next to him to examine his wound. The slash went across his chest, deep enough to lay open the flesh, but not enough to damage any internal organs.

"I'm not going to untie you, but I am going to bandage this up to slow down the bleeding."

"Why bother? Czernovitch is just going to kill me, anyway."

"No, he's not. You're going to live a long and healthy life. In prison." She glanced up at Rodion, who stood over them with his sword. "Prison, right?"

"Absolutely. I know a place built especially for his kind of people. Very safe and secure."

Rodion's smile was enough to frighten a sorcerer. Nazar paled and moaned.

Carina's bag had been left in the house, and Daria brought it out to her, flanked by Trick and Cole.

Touching him as little as possible, Carina and Rodion bound the old man's wound. Tired after the effort, Carina scooted away and sat back.

"There's more, right? Isn't there supposed to be a door?"

"You mean that door?" Trick pointed and she followed his gesture.

A free standing set of doors rose from the ground. Mist curled around the edges of the frame, showing nothing but wisps before they faded into the air.

Carina swallowed. "Ohh-kay. That doesn't look menacing at all."

It was so, so menacing.

And she was so tired. Rodion's touch had helped, but she was in more pain than she would let on. But she had to keep going because if she stopped, he would, too. Not because he felt obligated – at least, not that she could tell – but because he really seemed to care about her.

The feeling was mutual. And it wasn't the same feeling she'd had about him yesterday or last week, when she'd only admired him from afar because she thought he was good looking and mysterious. Now she knew so much more about him. She knew how he'd been injured, and how it had wounded him inside, beyond the physical. But she had also seen how he let in those who were close to him, how he loved his sister.

And she knew he had let her in, let her see him vulnerable and in pain, let her see him angry, and let her see him desiring her.

As the focus of that desire, she was very pleased that he

knew what he was doing. The little curl of heat in her belly revived her, making it easier to take a deep breath.

She pulled her bag close, but left her rope in Trick's hands.

"Ready, *milaya*?" asked Rodion, pulling her up by one hand.

"I guess I'd better be. Are you feeling all right?"

With his one strong hand, he kept pulling until she was pressed against him. "I'm better now."

"You keep calling me *milaya*. What does it mean?"

She'd never seen him blush before, but the tide of red that rushed up his neck and over his ears was probably the cutest thing she'd ever seen.

"It means *sweetheart*," called out Daria. "I think he likes you."

He took a deep breath, but didn't let her go. "I think sisters are a pain."

"We are," said his sister. "It's in the instruction manual."

"Does it say where there's a shut-off switch?"

Carina watched the siblings banter and breathed a quiet sigh of relief. It looked like Daria didn't object, which was great because she didn't want to lose her friend. Or her… whatever Rodion was.

She poked him gently in the side with a fingertip. "Sweetheart? So do I call you *milaya*, or is it different for men?"

"You would say *miliy*. And I would say *solnyshka, radast, angel moya*." His eyes burned with passion as he spoke. Russian had never sounded sexier.

"And as much fun as I'm having watching my brother fall for one of my best friends, there is a door here that's waiting for you."

Flame touched her arm at the reminder and she leaned back. "I think they're telling us it's time to go."

He leaned down and whispered into her ear. "We'll finish this later and I'll teach you more Russian."

She shivered at his warm breath against her neck. "Sounds good, *miliy*."

His eyes flashed. "Perfect. You'll be fluent in no time."

Her whole body gave an enthusiastic thumbs-up at that before she willed herself to settle down.

They faced the door together. "So... do we knock?"

"No need," he said, digging in his pocket. "We have a key. And a plan."

Chapter Eleven

Rodion pushed the door open with effort, the solid fir heavy and built to last. Built to absorb magic and repel those who weren't invited. Deep glossy red paint was trimmed in brilliant gilded detail – a reflection of nature, with fantastic animals not found in the mortal world. Unicorns, firebirds, domovoy, and leshy. Creatures both beautiful and terrifying, and some that were both. Artistic swirls and patterns dazzled the eye, drawing the attention, and with it, pulling down magical defenses.

He blinked and shook his head. "Don't look at the door too closely. It has magic of its own."

Carina nodded. She thought he hadn't noticed how much pain she was in. His brave woman. The lines around her mouth had deepened, her lips pale and pinched, but she made not a word of complaint. Even if she had, he would have admired her. After a day that had begun innocently with coffee, to have come so far with such a curse laid on her, she had earned the right to say whatever she wanted.

But she stood firm by his side and walked through the

door with him, armed with no more than a bag that held as much mystery as the room they walked into.

Like the nave of one of the onion-domed churches of his homeland, the space they entered soared above them. Columns lined the sides, the spaces there interspersed with fantastic statuary of magical beings like those depicted on the door, savage and lovely and cold. Each one was carved out of swirled pale marble, watching like ghosts.

"Are those real?" she whispered. "Are those statues, or are they... were they...?"

His gut clenched. They could be the work of a madly talented artist, but as he looked more closely, each one held the same look in their eyes – terror, horror, and pain. And every single one of them had swirls of black ink all over their bodies.

They weren't statues. They were living flesh made stone.

"Don't look, Carina. We're not here for them."

She nodded, but he saw the tears in her eyes, grief for the victims who had come before.

On the platform at the end of the nave, in front of the massive, wall-sized icons that depicted nothing holy, lay an altar. On top of the embroidered altar cloth lay a long pillow. And on that pillow, lay a sword.

Gebil. The sword wielded by Koschei the Deathless, who wished to rule over all the Rus on the fae side of the border he had guarded down in Volshev.

The sword was dedicated to death. Not conscious on its own, it still held the will of its master in its blade.

And he, apparently, had shards of it embedded in his bones.

"I suppose this at least explains some of the anger I've felt since my injury."

"Really? We all thought you were just having trouble dealing with it."

Magic's Fate

"I was. I admit that. But there were times when it felt like something was riding me. Pushing me to rages that left me exhausted and a little frightened."

Carina rested a hand on his arm. "I'm sorry. If I'd known, maybe I could have helped."

"I don't think so. I'm just glad there are only small shards in my bone. Anything bigger and I might have hurt you if you'd tried." He squeezed her hand lightly.

"So do we have a plan here, or are we winging it?"

He would have answered her, but he was interrupted.

A skeletal being draped in the rich robes of a king stepped out from behind the veiled Royal Door between the icons. His laugh echoed through the empty space, ringing strangely off the pillars and statues along the sides, filling the hollow dome above, before it fell back to them, having gathered emptiness on its travels.

He wore a tall crown, tufts of thin white hair sticking through the peaks. Flickering candlelight showed the jewels glinting dully through the film of smoke from the harsh incense that filled the air.

But his eyes reflected nothing. No light, no life. Nothing but neverending darkness.

"Have you brought what you stole from me?"

The words brought a painful chill to his skin, but he stepped forward. "I stole nothing, Lord Koschei. The pieces of Gebil were gifted to me."

"A hard gift."

"But a gift nonetheless."

"Then you will return it to me." The voice pierced his ears until he imagined he could feel blood running out of them.

Koschei was the stuff of terrifying childhood tales. He was the evil that would come and steal you in the night, take you away to eat you, drain away your life, and drink your blood so that he would never die. But Rodion hadn't been afraid of fairy stories for many years.

"You would steal it from me, Lord Koschei? Without honor? Without payment? Giving it back to you will come at a cost."

The one thing Rodion had learned from all those scary stories was that respect for powerful creatures in the Rus was paramount. No matter what position they occupied on the moral ladder, it was always a bad idea to be rude. But he also knew that if he didn't command respect for himself, he would lose the battle before it was ever fought.

The old man, his skin so thin his bones showed through, ran his fingers through his stringy beard.

"And what would you have as payment, young *bogatyr*?"

"The cure for a curse, my lord. Your servant, Nazar, placed the *proklyat'ye smerti* on this woman. I wish for it to be removed."

When those black eyes moved from him to Carina, Rodion felt as if a weight had been lifted from him. But then he immediately wanted it back. After all she'd been through, he wasn't sure Carina was up to the strain.

But she proved him wrong. Again.

He was going to have to get used to that.

She pulled herself up and looked Koschei the Deathless, the most fearsome entity in all the Rus fae – aside from Baba Yaga, herself – straight in the eye, and nodded.

"Show me your curse, seer."

She glanced over at Rodion, and he nodded. They had to show Koschei they were serious. At his gesture, she pulled up the sleeve of her shirt, although she hardly needed to. The deadly black ink covered her arm from shoulder to wrist, curling even over the back of her hand. And above the sleeve, the tendrils crawled up the side of her neck.

"Nazar does good work," chuckled the old monster.

Only the clutch of Carina's fingers on his arm held him back from striking Koschei. The madman noticed, and his chuckle became a cackle.

"I see why Nazar went for her, and not for you. Far more painful this way."

"He didn't go for her," he spat back. "He missed. We're only here because he missed."

"Either way, pain all around."

Rodion slashed the air abruptly with his hand. "Enough. We made it here. We fulfilled the terms of the curse. Now cure her."

"Ah, ah, ah." Koschei shook a bony finger at him. "You're not done yet. You have not yet returned the shards of Gebil."

The bony sorcerer stepped aside and spread his arm toward the altar.

A force like a giant hand wrapped around Rodion's body. The moment it touched him, he felt his power drain away, leaving him gasping at the emptiness inside. It drew him in, dropping him on the platform, in front of the raised table. He didn't even bother fighting. This was his destiny. His sacrifice so she would live.

He heard Carina cry out his name, and he twisted around to look back at her.

She was on her knees, one arm held out to him, and tears streaked her beautiful face. Tears for him. She'd done that too often today. Wept in pain because of him.

Desperate to give her something other than grief, he gave her the truth. "I love you, Carina. I'll make this right for you."

And then the pain took him.

In a haze of agony, he felt his arm burn as if someone was stabbing him with a red-hot poker.

He looked at his arm. Someone was stabbing it with a red-hot poker.

A hideous little being with leathery wings and too many teeth gleefully dug into his scar with a massive awl glowing with heat.

Rodion screamed. Blood poured down his arm as the hole the little monster was digging grew deeper. The smell of burning flesh seared his nostrils, triggering his gag reflex. He choked and coughed and held onto consciousness with everything he had.

And through the shreds of skin and muscle, three tiny specks rose. Crimson dripped off of them until they reflected a metallic glimmer in the candlelight.

The shards of Gebil that had been embedded in his arm during that fateful battle.

As if magnetized, they floated toward the sword, finding their place in the nicked blade. They settled in with an almost audible clang, and the sword... vibrated. It shimmered in a wave of darkness the color of spilled blood before it settled back onto the altar.

Rodion felt himself weakening. Even a *charodey* could die if he lost enough blood, and his was pumping out from the massive wound in his arm. It didn't matter. He'd made a promise to Carina to make this right, and he was going to keep it.

And the only way to fulfill that oath was to destroy the sword that had started it. He knew he couldn't kill Koschei. The man wasn't called "the Deathless" just because it sounded scary. His soul was hidden far beyond anything Rodion could find.

But Gebil was only a sword. Not an immortal.

Gathering everything that was left of his strength, he called out the phrase he'd taught Carina before they had walked through the door.

"Osvoboditye drakona!"

Silence filled the room, drowning out the last echo of his words. The creature drilling through his arm stopped digging and Koschei's grating laugh died off.

In their place, a whoosh of displaced air swept through the space, blowing out the candles and bringing with it the dry scent of a hot, clean desert breeze.

They saw the light before they heard the scream. And they heard the scream before they felt the heat.

The dragon's wings blocked out all light except what came from his muzzle, brilliant and golden, touched with red.

Gebil was caught directly in the heart of the dragonfire. For long moments, it withstood the heat, slowly beginning to glow until it added its own heat to the conflagration. Brighter and brighter it shone until it began to consume itself. Flames arose from the blade as it warped and melted, the metal oozing its way down the altar to pool on the floor. There, the liquid boiled and bubbled until it turned to steam and ash.

When the last bit of it blew away on hot air, it was as if a vacuum of power was released. A sonic blast of magic exploded through the room, highlighting the dragon that took up most of the space in the castle before it faded away.

The prized sword of Koschei the Deathless was no more.

Rodion tried to roll away, but flame kissed his bleeding arm, burning away nerve endings until he felt heat but no pain.

His minuscule torturer turned to ash in a blink. Koschei's robes were in flames, and the fire reflected the evil in the old man's eyes. The clothing burned away, and his skeletal figure, still monstrously strong, was revealed. He stood within the fire and laughed again. Not an old man's weak cackle, but a boom.

"I fulfilled my end of the deal, Lord Koschei," called out Rodion. "Uphold your honor!"

Koschei sneered. "We'll play this game again, *Charodey* Czernovitch. If there's anything left of you to play with."

"No," he whispered. He didn't have anything left to bring back the evil wizard. Carina would die.

And it would be his fault.

Chapter Twelve

Carina had never even let a cat out of the bag, much less a dragon, so when Rodion called out the signal, she had opened the bag made from the weave of her life. Ivan Tsvetkov, retired MMA fighter and dragon shifter, stepped out. She'd laughed weakly.

"Can you imagine what would happen if I spilled the beans?"

The massive, bald man she'd met less than an hour ago, had looked at her strangely, but she'd waved away his concern.

"Sorry. Weird sense of humor. I'll die and my last words will be a terrible pun."

The man snorted and shifted, his dragon form snorting a gout of flame before he turned away to do his job, which was to melt the evil sword.

After they got Nazar sorted and taken away, there had been only one thing left to do. Get the shards back to the sword, and exchange that service for Carina's cure.

It had sounded so easy. So clean and simple. Yes, the

timing would be tricky, but she hadn't allowed herself to think much beyond that.

Asking for Ivan's help had been the easiest thing they'd done all day. The giant Russian fighter had shown up at Daria's house with his girlfriend, and he'd immediately agreed to putting a spike in Koschei's wheels.

"I remember the stories of Koschei the Deathless. I thought I'd left them behind in Russia, but evil goes wherever it can creep, *da*? Of course I will help."

He'd barely blinked when they'd asked him to climb into Carina's totebag. No one thought he'd be able to fit his toe inside, much less anything else. But as he stepped in with the other foot, his eyes had widened when he fit without even touching the edges. Monalisa had unsuccessfully stifled a giggle as she watched her giant boyfriend disappear into a handbag.

"Now that is some handy magic, girl. Where can I get one?"

Carina had just smiled mysteriously, closed the bag and slung it over her shoulder as if it weighed almost nothing.

Their plan had worked. Mostly. Rodion was dead. They hadn't discussed it, but they both knew that if he ended up anywhere near that altar when Ivan did his thing, he wouldn't survive the dragonflame.

And she'd known she wasn't walking out of there alive. She'd shown Rodion where the ink had spiraled over her arm and neck, but she hadn't let him see where it ate deeper into her body, consuming her bit by bit. Her blood burned like acid as it pumped through her body.

But Gebil was destroyed, and that was important. The plan had mostly worked.

Now she lay on the floor of an evil castle filled with the dead creature statues that would keep her body company throughout eternity, and she was glad she'd never have to hear Rodion scream like that ever again. No pain anymore for him. For either of them.

An explosion of magic rolled over her when the sword died. The black stopped its toxic spread, but it was too late. Her heart bumped weakly in her chest and the effort it took to breathe was hardly worthwhile.

She couldn't see what was happening on the altar with a giant dragon's butt in her way, so she let herself rest. There was nothing left to do now. The sword was gone. Rodion had kept his promise to make this right.

A movement off to the side caught her eye. In the back, someone seriously skinny and alarmingly naked scurried away from the flames. Koschei. She wondered how he'd survived, then remembered that he was, after all, "the Deathless." When Rodion had outlined the plan, sorry, the "mission parameters," as he'd called them. When he'd done that, Koschei's death wasn't on the list. They'd been concerned with the sword, so really, it had all worked out. But she didn't want her last vision on this earth to be that awful man's scrawny butt, so she turned her head to the other side.

The statues were moving. Life flowed over them, melting away the cold marble and the black poison swirls like water pouring out of a mountain spring. She smiled and let her mind float with the pretty hallucination.

A lady with green, leafy things in her hair came to kneel beside Carina. And someone who looked like a friendly Sasquatch. A big frog man stared at her, then hopped wetly away. He hadn't looked very pleasant, but she told herself it wasn't right to judge people... frog men... on their appearance. Maybe frog ladies thought he was hot.

She was glad they weren't trapped anymore. They were going to be all right.

She rolled her head back to see what was happening, but

there was still a dragon there. He wasn't breathing fire anymore, though. That was just regular fire, burning down the castle.

Carina almost smiled. Not her circus, not her monkeys. Not anymore. Rodion was already gone and she was going to be with him, wherever they ended up.

She wasn't even in pain anymore, which was pleasant, since she'd been hurting all day. All she wanted to do was lay here for a little while until it was over. Instead, someone gently scooped her up and put her down on something warm and slightly furry and moving.

Not quite how she'd planned on going, but it was all out of her hands now. Carina closed her eyes and quietly, she died.

Chapter Thirteen

They needed a bigger bed, decided Rodion.

He lay next to Carina on the queen-sized mattress in his sister's guest room, and decided that when they were married, they would need something bigger than this.

He had awakened a while ago, but didn't want to move yet. It felt too good to be alive, lying next to the woman he loved.

He spent the time arguing with himself.

What kind of idiot fell in love in a day? Obviously, *he* was that kind of idiot. He'd known Carina for a while. He had liked her and thought her pretty before when he was broken, but he wasn't broken anymore. Or was he? Normal people didn't go from "Hey, you're kind of cute" to "Please bear my children" in less than twenty-four hours. Not that they were normal people. Maybe it was different for the magical. After all, Daria and Trick had been inseparable since the day they met.

So was this love, or just infatuation? How did he know that this feeling wouldn't fade now that the excitement and danger were gone? He couldn't be sure, he supposed, but as he studied her beautiful face and the tendrils of bright pink and purple that threaded through her hair, this didn't feel like a whim.

For one, she was too strong and solid to inspire something as lukewarm as a whim. The moment he'd let himself, the thin thread of attraction he'd let himself feel before had swelled into a lifeline. He could feel her connected to the solid center of him. She was woven into his magic, his blood, his life.

He had told her he loved her yesterday. Technically, he'd shouted it as he was pulled to certain death by an evil fae lord, but in the clear, quiet light of early morning, with the sun gently breaking through the gray of dawn, would she believe it was still true? And most of all, did she love him, too?

She stirred, her long limbs stretching, her toes brushing his knee. They'd been icy cold last night. As exhausted as he'd been when he fell into bed beside her, their touch on his leg had still made him gasp before he trapped her frozen feet between his calves and suffered until they warmed up.

She rolled onto her side, facing him, and he copied her movement so they were face to face.

Her eyes opened. She smiled.

"I found you," she whispered. "I'm so glad. I wasn't looking forward to having to search for you from one end of Heaven to the other."

"What?"

"We're dead. I mean, it kind of sucks because I thought I'd have more time to accomplish things, but we're dead together, so that's all right."

Warmth spread through Rodion.

She definitely loved him.

He draped his right arm carefully over her waist and

pulled her closer. "Would you be really disappointed if I told you we weren't dead?"

"Oh, honey." She hugged him. "We're definitely dead. Ivan fried you. I saw it. And you're healed, see?" She pointed to his shoulder. "That wouldn't happen if you were live."

A thin, pink line and a lick of slick, supple scar tissue next to it in the shape of dragon's wings were the only reminders left of the wound that had caused him such pain for so long. He wasn't sure when it had happened, only that it was done. With the shards gone, there was no reason for the pain he'd felt to linger. The nerve and muscle and bone destroyed by digging out the shards of Gebil had regenerated as if by magic.

All right. Definitely by magic. Just like Carina. They'd been operating under the assumption that Koschei held the cure to her curse. In fact, the curse had only said that once they fulfilled the quests, she would be healed, whether Koschei was there or not.

He thanked everything on earth, above and below, because Koschei had slithered out of the burning castle like his bony butt was on fire. Which it was.

Rodion had lain in front of that altar of the damned and hoped death would come quickly. Since the moment he'd been wounded, he had compared the pain in his shoulder to fire.

The touch of dragonflame made his previous agony seem like a papercut.

He'd been sure he was hallucinating when a double-headed eagle picked him up in its claws and glided low to the ground out of the smoke-filled castle. If he was going to be eaten by something, he supposed his end could be worse than to be consumed by the regal symbol of his homeland.

But he hadn't been eaten. Instead, the eagle had followed a

very large, bald man out of the castle. A man whose eyes glowed golden, and whose skin shimmered with the hint of scales.

Over the back of a white horse, he'd seen another form. Carina, slumped over and motionless. He was not ashamed to say that he'd wept.

Now he flexed his fingers. "Yes, I'm healed. And so are you."

She pulled up her hand and looked at it. Free of any tattoos or traces of black, her unblemished skin glowed in the pearly light of dawn.

"Good. I hope my body actually looks like this because my mama is going to pitch a fit if she sees me covered in that tattoo."

Okay. This was not going quite the way he'd intended. Carina was stubborn. He tried again.

"But *milaya*, we're not dead."

"How do you know?" she asked.

"Because we're in Daria's guest room."

With a frown, she pushed her way up. "What? What are we doing here?"

"Ivan and the others brought us out of Koschei's house before it burned. You have made a number of new friends."

She shook her head, different colored curls bouncing. "This doesn't make sense. I was prepared to die. I thought I was dead."

"Nope." He crossed his arms behind his head and lay back to watch her. "We're alive."

"We're alive," she repeated. Then said it again. "We're alive." Her face beaming, she turned and straddled him, taking him by the shoulders, laughing and shaking him. At least, she tried to shake him. It tickled.

He laughed with her, free and completely happy for the first time in far too long.

And then he wasn't laughing anymore because Carina leaned down and kissed him as though she intended to do it for a very long time. Because she loved him.

She loved him. She adored him, in fact. Carina was sure, in the back of her mind, that he would eventually do something that would make her want to whack him with a skillet, but it didn't matter. It wouldn't matter. They'd been through so much already that even if he left his wet towels on the floor, they'd work through it.

But right at this moment, she didn't want to stop anything.

Her hair slipped over her shoulder and it didn't smell like her shampoo. "Did someone give me a bath?"

He held her straddled over him with his big hands planted on her thighs, and answered. "Daria and Katya did. You were unconscious, but they got you clean and dressed you before putting you to bed." He tugged at the bottom hem of a massively oversized t-shirt featuring a handsome man on the cover of a book by Roxy St. James. She had one like it at home – with a different hero from a different book – that was a memento of a book signing by a now-local romance writer.

The one thing her friends hadn't provided was a change of undergarments. Looked like she was free-wheelin' it today. This discovery was... inspiring.

"I notice that you are also in this bed."

His hands continued to toy with the hem of the shirt. "That's true. They must have run out of room. When space is tight, sometimes you have to double up."

"Is that right?"

She'd never seen Rodion actually flirt before, and she wondered if he'd been such a charmer before his injury. Either way, it was really cute.

"Basic survival skills. You have to cuddle to survive the cold weather."

"It's May. In Georgia."

"You know Daria. She keeps the AC turned up way too high."

Carina laughed quietly. She didn't want to wake anyone up, after all. "I expect you'd know all about how to survive these freezing temperatures."

"I do," he answered. Then he paused, and his face became serious. "With love. Carina, I know I told you yesterday that I loved you. And you may think it's too soon."

She shook her head, but he put a thick, calloused finger to her lips. "Don't answer yet. Let me get this out first."

He was so serious that she had to work hard to contain her smile. Could he be more adorable?

"But I want to be with you, and I hope you want to be with me, too."

She wasn't laughing anymore. This was a man who'd just laid his heart bare for her. She hadn't left him on his own yesterday, and she sure wasn't going to start now.

Carina reached down and laced her fingers through his.

"I don't think there's any timeline on love. I may not be ready to say it back to you yet, but this thing that I feel for you." She pulled their hands together between her breasts and held them there. "What I feel is real and solid and good. And I'm more than willing to work it out with you. Is that okay? Is that enough?"

Rodion untangled their fingers and slide his up to bury them in her hair. "It's more than enough. But, *milaya*?"

"Yes, *miliy*?"

"I do love you."

He pulled her down for a kiss that left her feeling like a heatwave had hit. She leaned over and whispered a few words in his ear, making sure to brush her fingers along his broad, lightly furred chest, over his wide shoulders, and down his very, very nice six-pack. He responded to her suggestions with great, and skilled, enthusiasm.

Carina Valdis had never been so happy to be alive.

After a long morning of exploring their wildly blooming relationship, they finally rolled out of the rumpled bed, took turns in the shower – she liked Daria's house a lot, but she was sure Heaven would have nicer showers – and left their room to discover far too many people eyeing them indulgently over cups of coffee.

Ivan rose from the table to refill his plate with a mountain of bacon and eggs, and whacked Rodion on the back on his return trip.

"Good to see you both lived."

Rodion rolled his shoulder with a slight grimace, then smiled. "Thanks to you, *moy drog*. We couldn't have done it without you."

The giant shrugged and said, "I only came in to, how do you say, clean up the bat?"

"I think he means 'bat clean up.'" Trick was plowing his way through his fair share of breakfast, too, and Rodion grabbed a plate and joined in.

Carina poured herself a cup of coffee and leaned against the counter. Caffeine first, then food.

"Thanks for letting us stay, Daria." She wasn't quite sure how to approach her friend. It was one thing, she supposed, to know your brother and your bestie were making googly eyes at each other. It was another for them to, er, google their eyes in your guest room. But Daria was taking it all in stride, checking the oven to see if the next rack of bacon was done.

"And where else were you going to go? Trust me, there is not enough room in your building for what you brought back."

Carina lifted an eyebrow. "I'm sorry, what?"

Daria pointed to the sliding glass door that led to the back yard.

A unicorn was eating the petals off Daria's newly planted roses.

"I'd be more upset about the roses, but...unicorn!"

Carina stared, her coffee forgotten in her hand. "I don't understand."

Their friend Katya, who ran a shelter for both regular and supernatural animals, but could barely work up the courage to talk to the check-out clerk at the grocery store, opened the slider and stuck her head in. She smelled of warm spices and... oh. Ew.

This time, Daria did shriek. "If you're coming in, take off your shoes. Don't you track that smell into my house."

Katya waved dismissively. "Your firebird is building a nest above the garage. We're going to need more cinnamon sticks."

Daria and Carina looked at each other, then back at Katya, and shook their heads.

"Firebirds build their nests from cinnamon sticks before they immolate themselves. She needs more for a good nest."

"No. She's not nesting on my garage, then setting herself on fire." Daria charged out the door, Katya hard on her heels, and started yelling at a large, red and gold bird perched on the roof. Everyone else drifted outside to watch – Trick carried his plate and fork out with him – leaving Carina and Rodion in the house.

"I thought my life would get more normal as I got older," she said. "Soothsayers don't usually have days like yesterday."

"*Milaya*, I don't think most people have days like yesterday on a regular basis. Not even Border Crossing agents."

"Speaking of Border Crossing agents, now that you're

healed, are you going to go back to Volshev and get your job back?"

He stood behind her and wrapped his arms around her waist, pulling her flush to his body. He felt amazing. Right. Perfect, actually. She tried to stay calm as she waited for him to answer.

"I don't know. If I'd been cured two days ago, I'd be gone already. But right now? I don't know. I do still have a few more weeks of leave to use."

Rodion turned her around in his embrace until she faced him. "Carina, I want to be with you. Whether that's going back to Volshev to be an agent again, staying here in Nocturne Falls to do something else, or some other option entirely, I want to be where you are."

With a small cry, she wrapped her arms around his chest and squeezed as hard as she could. "Me, too, Rodion. Wherever we are, let's be together."

"I have to say, it will be nice getting to know you better without any curses hanging over us. And we don't have to make any decisions right now." He looked out the door. "Although, I think we might have to decide not to allow any firebirds to nest on our building's roof."

"Good decision."

Epilogue

THE KELPIE

*B*ubba decided that if he couldn't get Honeycrisps or Braeburns, then these little Piñata apples would do. Of course, he'd torn Rodion's sleeve for bringing them, purely on principle. It wouldn't do for people to start thinking he'd accept less than the best apples.

Life was pretty good here in Nocturne Falls. He liked Wolf Creek. He liked being with Trick and Daria, who came out and swam with him on most nights. He especially enjoyed riding with Carina, who had a lot of experience with mortal horses. She spoke to him of the human competitions she called rodeos and, although it sounded like fun, he still preferred his stretch of water here.

It would be nice to have a little non-human/non-*rusalka* company, though. Another who could run with him. Who could be part of his herd.

A sound had him pricking up his ears. He didn't see anything, but he could hear and smell the source. Something was trying to come near. After a moment, he spotted it. Her. Another horse, but not a mortal one. She was a fae creature, like him.

She was beautiful. Small and delicate. Not big and rangy and black with water weeds in her mane, like him. Although he thought the water weeds made him a very handsome kelpie. Instead, she was so white she glowed, and the long, sharp horn on her head pulsed with life and magic.

She walked up to him hesitantly, her head high, ready to wheel and run if he struck out at her.

But he'd never do that to her. Instead, he put his nose down and rolled one of his precious apples in her direction.

After a moment, she dropped her head and lipped at his offering, before picking it up and crunching through the fruit.

Now he had a herd. Life was good.

Acknowledgments

Writing may be a solitary endeavor, but producing a book for people to read can't be done alone.

Editing: Theresa Cole

Beta Reader: Donna Simmonds

Cover Design: Jax Cassidy, Keri Knutson, Rebecca Poole

Formatting: Emily Robertson

Thanks especially go to Kristen Painter for inviting me to play in her world, as well as over all awesomeness.

Any factual mistakes made are my fault alone, despite the excellent advice of everyone (thank you, LimeCello!) who helped me along the way. I also can't thank Yelena Casale enough for taking the time to be so patient with all my questions about the Russian language. She's a gem!

The Chatzy team kept me focused during the craziness of writing and blurb-crafting, and too many others to mention were invaluable along the way.

And last, but not least, ***thank you to my family***, who have rallied behind me at every turn. They're amazing and I love them.

About the Author

Sela Carsen was born into a traveling family, then married a military man to continue her wandering lifestyle. With her husband of 20+ years, their two teens, her mother, the dogs, and the cat, she's finally (temporarily) settled in the Midwest. Between bouts of packing and unpacking, she writes paranormal and sci-fi romances, with or without dead bodies. Your pick.

Subscribe to my newsletter and you'll always know what's coming up!

SelaCarsen.com

Other Books Available

Nocturne Falls Universe:
Light Paranormal Romance set in Kristen Painter's Nocturne Falls
Magic's Song
Magic's Fate
Magic's Promise
Magic's Frost - in the Merry & Bright anthology

Wolves of Fenrir series:
Sci-Fi Shifter Romance with a healthy dose of Vikings
A Wolf to Watch Over Me
A Most Wanted Wolf
Silver Wolf Rising
The Wolf Who Came In From the Cold

Carolina Wolf series:
Paranormal Romance with sexy, steamy, Southern werewolves
Carolina Wolf
Carolina Pearl

Legends and Lore stories:
Stand alone Fantasy and Paranormal Romances with mythology and folklore.
The Sleeper Dreamed: A Short Story
Runespell
Not Quite Dead
Heart of the Sea

Made in the USA
Lexington, KY
11 September 2018